THE HOOD WAS BACK!
My name's Ryan, but people call me
"Irish" or—"the Hood" . . .

I had walked into one hell of a mess.
Big Step thought I had knocked off his
brother, and I had had the motive, the
ability and the time to do it.

The cops wanted me, too. I'd been in
their hair too damn long, and they'd
love to see me take a fall.

And then there was Karen Sinclair, the
most beautiful dame I'd ever seen.
She picked me out of a crowd—because
she'd seen the ruthless look of a killer
in my eyes, and she needed a man like me!

MICKEY SPILLANE IN TOP FORM
—with two slick, swift novels
as tough as they come:

RETURN OF THE HOOD and
THE BASTARD BANNERMAN

Also by MICKEY SPILLANE

VENGEANCE IS MINE
MY GUN IS QUICK
ONE LONELY NIGHT
THE BIG KILL
THE LONG WAIT
I, THE JURY
KISS ME, DEADLY
THE DEEP
ME, HOOD!
THE GIRL HUNTERS
THE FLIER

and published by CORGI BOOKS

MICKEY SPILLANE

RETURN OF THE HOOD

CORGI BOOKS
A DIVISION OF TRANSWORLD PUBLISHERS

RETURN OF THE HOOD

A CORGI BOOK

First publication
in Great Britain

PRINTING HISTORY
Corgi Edition published 1964

Copyright © Transworld Publishers Ltd., 1964

Corgi Books are published by Transworld Publishers Ltd.,
Bashley Road, London, N.W.10.
Made and printed in Great Britain by
Hunt, Barnard & Co., Ltd., Aylesbury, Bucks.

RETURN OF THE HOOD

Chapter 1

Newbolder and Schmidt were decent about it. They came in, nodded and sat down at their table with coffee in front of them and let me alone to finish my supper. Sometimes you just can't figure cops. But once they made their touch, there was no sense running. Try it and you can get shot down. Go along with the game and you have a chance. Besides, the Cafeteria was a popular place and the owner a swell egg who didn't deserve getting shook by a big punch right in the middle of his rush hour.

So I nodded back and let them know I was ready when I cleaned my plate and that there wouldn't be any fireworks or tough talk no matter how big the beef was. And it was a big beef. Real big. I was a murder suspect and in a way it was lucky the cops made the scene first because in the same neighborhood the Stipetto brothers were canvassing the area for me too and with them it meant playing guns.

With them I could play. I had a .45 calibre instrument that could sound off loud and clear, but with cops you don't play like that. On somebody else the fuzz would have stepped up and made the pinch without waiting. For this one time I had to be an exception because of what happened a year ago, and for that they were being decent. Something like General Arnold's boot if you got enough smarts to know what I mean.

The cops didn't watch me. I was there, part of their peripheral vision, they weren't in any hurry at all and were glad to sit in out of the rain and the cold for a few minutes. They had the faces of cops all over the world that you can't miss if you're in the business on one side or the other.

Across the room with his back to the wall, Wally Pee who ran numbers for Sal Upsidion started to sweat and couldn't finish what was on his tray. He kept glancing from Newbolder and Schmidt to Izzy Goldwitz, who was at the counter getting seconds, because Izzy had six grand in cash in the overnight bag he carried and with Sal Upsidion you didn't give any excuses if it didn't get turned in. When Izzy paid the cashier and started back he caught Wally's signal and turned white, but by then it was too late to do anything except finish supper, so he sat down and tried to bluff it out.

I could have gone over and told them, but it didn't make any difference anyway and for them it was better to sweat a little so that the next time they'd be on their toes more. Newbolder's quick case of the place didn't make them since I was his target and not much else mattered, so the numbers boys were off the hook for this time, anyway.

Funny, funny.

New York after dark, a vivid chameleon who by day was a roaring scaly dragon of business and ceremony, and by night a soft quivering thing because the guts of the city had gone home leaving the shell to be invaded by parasites.

The few who stayed, and the tourists, kept to the Gay White Way as they used to name it, clubbing, bar hopping or taking in a show. But the perimeter of life had closed down to the very heart of the city. Beyond the perimeter was where the dying came. A few arteries of light and life extended crosstown, went up a ways and down a ways, but that was all. The great verdant cancer of Central Park was like a sparkling jewel, laced with the multicolor of taxis whose beams probed ahead of them with twin fingers, always searching. Like Damocles.

Around me the restaurant was packed with people from Jersey, Brooklyn, the Island, all getting ready to go home or take in the town a little. The regulars were there too, the handful of natives whose home was Manhattan no matter what. Some were night people like me and Wally Pee and Izzy; the others came because the food was good and inexpensive.

I wondered what my chances were on the rap. They didn't look good at all.

Somebody had knocked off Penny Stipetto. Two days before I had belted his ass from one end of 45th and Second all the way to the next corner for shaking down Rudy Max and when he healed up he strapped on a rod and went looking for me with a skinful of big H to keep his courage up.

Word travels fast in this town. I got the news and passed it back that I was ready and available any time, any place and if I saw him first he was going to get laid out.

Trouble was, I didn't see him first.

Somebody else did and they found Penny Stipetto wedged behind a couple of garbage cans two blocks away from my pad with a hole in his head.

That was enough for the remaining brothers Stipetto. They spread out a net across the city that was as efficient as any the fuzz could throw and pulled the strings tight until I only had one block to run in and one place to go.

The condemned man ate a hearty meal.

Hell, I was *glad* Newbolder and Schmidt found me first. This was the age of enlightened crime and a gang shoot out comes only of immediate necessity. Revenge is a thing of the past except for the extreme occasion, and if the law will do the job equally as well, then let it go, man. In fact, the brothers Stipetto would only be too happy to help the fuzz nail my hide. They'd make damn sure *somebody* saw me in the area at the time Penny took

9

the big slide and damn sure any alibi I had would fold if they had to remove it forever.

In other words, I was a dead duck. I had no alibi to begin with unless a warm solo pad could be called one, the hole in Penny's head was big enough to be made by at least a .45 and no spent slug was recovered for comparison. I had the motive, the time, a probable weapon and on top of it all, the critical, anti-social personality that, according to the psycho meds, made such a deed possible.

In short, I was a hood.

Newbolder sipped his coffee and glanced at his watch. He wasn't rushing me, but I knew he'd like to get off his shift on time and a cop can only be decent so long. By then Wally Pee and Izzy Goldswitz had caught the pitch and were begging me with their eyes to get the hell out before the two cops decided to case the place for any other interesting characters and spotted them.

Let them take care of themselves, I thought, and went back to the Hungarian goulash. It was good and there was no telling when I'd be getting another plate of the stuff.

I had almost finished when the broad sat down. Like they'll always do, she sat down directly opposite me rather than at the side, trying to make out as if she had the table all to herself. I knew she was an out-of-towner when she ate without taking the dishes off her tray, something a cafeteria regular never would do.

There was something odd about her I couldn't place, but in New York you don't stare too long or take deliberate second looks because privacy is a funny thing, like the props in theatre-in-the-round. Privacy exists because you pretend nothing else is there and in a chow joint you're expected to obey the rules of the game.

But I couldn't help the second look. I made it as surreptitious as possible and found the flaw. The tall girl with the deep chestnut hair was made up to perfection, if perfection meant deliberately disguising a classic beauty to become just another fairly pretty dame worth smiling at sometimes, but not much more.

They do that sometimes. Broads get screwy ideas about their looks and plenty of times I've seen real treats done up in trick suits in the beatnik shops.

Who are you today, honey—Hepburn? You could be LaMarr if you liked. You have a luscious mouth with the kind of pouty lips that can kiss like crazy but the lipstick is wrong. That eyebrow pencil accent is way off too. Way off. And you can't quite erase genes that put a tricky, exotic slant in your eyes and cheekbones with cleverly applied green shadows and too-pale makeup.

When she strugged the white trench coat off, I saw it was only her face that had been changed to the mediocre. Nothing could have been done to alter the magnificence of her body. There was just too much of her, just too much big, lovely much.

The condemned man ate a hearty meal. Visually, that is.

So while they waited for me, those outside watching to make sure those inside didn't slip, I feasted a little bit and knew I was wearing a crooked grin that couldn't be helped but could be hidden if I chewed hard enough.

Newbolder had shifted his seat a little so he could see around the broad, not giving up his cop's habits for any reason, and I finished my goulash and started in on my pie.

It was just a voice. It was strangely low, detached and was there without seeming to come from any one point. It was almost totally lost in the grand hum of voices that kept the room in motion and for a second I couldn't place it.

When I did I kept on eating, doing a quick think because it was the broad speaking to me con style without moving her lips or changing her expression, and all the while managing to eat as if she were completely alone.

"Can you talk without looking at me?"

In my racket you learn to play by ear real fast or get dead real fast and I had nothing to lose at all any more.

So I said, "Go ahead, honey," and like her, my mouth didn't move either except to eat.

The broad caught it immediately and said, "You did time?" and there was a hesitancy in her voice.

"No. Not quite. The fuzz would like me to go down though."

"Service record?"

That was a peculiar angle for a new line to take. I was trying to figure her for a high class hooker or a tomato with a hot item for sale, but this bit threw the picture out of focus. I did a mental shrug and said, "A whole war, kid, but that was sixteen years ago." I half-laughed and smothered it. "Even got a few medals out of it."

"I'm in trouble."

"It figures," I said.

She buttered a piece of roll, bit off a bite and glanced vacantly around the room. I cut into my pie with my fork and concentrated on my last meal.

"You'll have to help," she finally got out.

I swallowed and forked out another bit of pie. "Why?"

"You're the only one who looks capable."

"Of what?"

She lifted her coffee cup and sipped at it. "Killing somebody if you have to."

This time it wasn't so easy to swallow the pie. I kept chewing, wondering why the hell I always drew the loonies. Sooner or later they always wind up in my lap. "Come off it, baby," I told her softly.

She didn't try to argue about it. She made it a square, simple statement that put her either way out or close inside and left me right in the middle no matter what happened.

She said, "My name is Karen Sinclair. I'm a government agent working with *Operation Hightower*. In my mouth I have a capsule containing a strip of microfilm that must be delivered to the head of our bureau at once. It's a matter of national safety. *Is that clear? National security is involved.* I'm going to bite into a roll, push it inside and put the rest of the roll down. When I leave you pick that roll up and get it in the hands of the nearest F.B.I. agent. Can you do that?"

"Sure." It was all I could think of to say. It still wasn't making sense. Finally, I added, "What's the act for?"

Unconcernedly, she said, "Because outside there are three men who are going to kill me to get that capsule back and we can't let it happen."

I was almost done with my pie and couldn't stall much longer. Newbolder and Schmidt were getting impatient. "More, baby."

With an involuntary gesture, she bit her lip, remembered in time to fake it and sipped at her coffee again. "They were almost ready to take me on the street. They know I have no contact here and am headed for a certain point so they suppose I really stopped to eat. What they don't realize is that I spotted them."

"Look, if you're serious. . . ."

"I'm serious." Her voice was the same flat monotone, yet had a new note to it, quiet and deadly. She wasn't lying.

"Hell, girl, I can . . ."

"You can do nothing, mister. If you want to help do as you're told. That's the only way this information can be passed on to the right people. You're the only chance I have. I know what I'm up against. I've been in this game a long time too and knew the odds when I started. I hate to have to pass this to amateurs but when I picked you it was because you had all the signs of the kind of man who can live outside the law and still hang on to certain principles. I hope I'm right."

She picked up a roll, broke it in half and nibbled into it. What she did, she did quickly, putting the remainder of the roll back on the plate, then washing it down with the rest of her coffee. She finished quickly without seeming to be in a hurry, put her arms back into the trench coat, belted it and picked up her pocketbook.

Before she left I felt her eyes scan my face briefly and sensed the greenish heat of them.

"Thanks," she said, then turned and walked away.

Indifferently, I picked the half a roll up, dunked it in my coffee, and chewed into it. The capsule was a brittle plastic against my teeth and when I wiped my mouth I spit it out in my hand and quietly stuck it in my watch pocket, then finished the roll.

If it was a gag, it was a beauty.

If it wasn't, then there was big trouble happening too fast for me to think out.

Newbolder stood up and so did I. It was about that time and now I was going to have the blocks put to me but good. Both cops knew I had the .45 on me and although they knew it was there for the Stipetto crowd they didn't take the big chance and kept their hands held just-so right above their Police Specials. This one time they'd play it neat all the way to the squad car for old time's sake and after that all bets were off.

I put on my hat, picked up my coat when two shots blew the night apart outside and a great blast tore the window out of the restaurant and scattered fragments all over the place. Women screamed as though they were given a downbeat and tables overturning in the sudden rush away from the front were like the crashing cymbals of a mad symphony.

I saw Newbolder and Schmidt pull at their guns and

14

run for the door as another handful of shots were triggered off and in that one instant the door was open as they ran through I saw the big girl falling against a car at the curb while the gun in her hand pointed at something out of sight and spouted tiny red flashes.

The decision wasn't mine at all. She had made it for me. I did the same thing everybody else did and ran, letting the crowd cover me. There was only one difference. I knew where I was running. I got to the door leading to the dishwashing section, went through quickly and paused, looking for another exit. I spotted it down the end, took a fast look through the small window in the door behind me and knew that it was no kind of a gag at all. A harmless looking rabbity guy whom I had unconsciously noticed trying to come across the room against the fleeing crowd had reached my table and was going through the remnants around the girl's plate. He finished, made a gesture toward where I had been sitting and stopped, then looked around thoughtfully and followed the crowd toward the main kitchen doors.

I would have liked it if he had come in beside me, but he hadn't as yet. He would, but I wasn't going to wait.

Any broad that would go all the way out, even knowing she was going to get hit, just to deliver a small package, needed a hand up. I fingered out the capsule and looked at it for the first time. It was transparent and inside was a packed white powder. Clever. It could appear to be a medicine. But there was a faint pinpoint of dark against the plastic where a corner of hidden microfilm touched it. I grinned, put it back in my pocket and took off for the doorway.

It swung out into a corridor lit by a single overhead bulb. By the exit doorway was a light switch I flicked off so I wouldn't step out silhouetted against a bright room.

My precautions almost worked.

Almost. Not quite.

There was a funny *shock* you hear rather than feel when metal hits bone and an overwhelming stuffiness began to smother me and I knew that I hadn't made it after all.

Chapter 2

All right, I thought, where the hell am I now? I realized I was conscious without first experiencing sight or sound, a peculiar awareness that was common to a person coming out of a deep sleep. I lay there a moment, deliberately thoughtful, concentrating on the moment, trying to retrieve my last hours of remembrance.

They came with the physical sensation of restriction and with a sudden jolt I felt the ropes that bit into my ankles and wrists. I was sitting up, hands and legs tied to a chair, my mouth open slackly and my head hanging forward limply. For a while I stayed like that, watching my feet and thinking. Just thinking.

From behind me the girl said, "Why did you bring him here, Fly? You crazy?"

A nervous, slimey voice said, "Maybe you got a better idea? Why you think Big Step made me stay back there. He figured this guy might pull something and he sure did. That he sure did."

"Big Step didn't want him here. He wasn't going to bring him here. They was supposed to go someplace in Jersey."

"Sure they was, but who knew this punk had guns around? Outside he had two guys and a broad who started shooting up then Carl and Moe figured they was part of this guy's bunch and cut loose at 'em. Then them two cops come outa the joint and everything goes to hell, like. Man, ain't nothing like that since that business in Havana before Castro."

"I don't care," the girl insisted," you better take him someplace else."

"Not me, Lisa, not me. You think Big Step won't want him even more now? First Penny dead, now Little Step and Carl and Moe. Big Step, he's gonna wanta carve on this here punk now for sure and whoever puts him outa reach is in for it."

"Listen, Fly, first thing the fuzz does is look around Big Step's places and that means the first thing they come here. This looks good with him here? Big Step wants a kidnapping rap besides? Maybe he can cover for the shooting . . . he woulda been somewhere else while it was going on, but this he won't hold still for."

The one called Fly pushed back a chair and walked around the room. I knew the guy. He was a cheap hood from the east side who did errands for the Stipetto brothers and lived off the white *Horse* he peddled around the neighborhood. He was his own best customer.

"So what'll I do?"

Lisa said, "Go bring up a car. We can get him over back of the store until we hear from Big Step."

Fly was glad to have somebody else make the decision. He grunted an acknowledgment, came over to me and yanked my head up. I kept my eyes closed and played it cute.

He said "You awake, Ryan? Come on, Punk. Up. Wake up." He gave me a backhand across the jaw that didn't do much except make me put down another mental mark in his dead book. "Quit stallin', Ryan. Yoy hear me?"

"Let him be," Lisa cut in. "You sapped him pretty hard."

"Damn right I did. This boy carries a big piece. You see that .45 I took off'n him?"

"I saw it," Lisa said, her tone bored.

"He had a cap of H on him too. You know that?"

This time Lisa sounded more interested. "Him? I didn't know this big coot blasted any?"

"He carried it. In his watch pocket."

"Well, he always was a nervy guy. So now we know. He's like all the rest. Got to get his nerve up a vein."

"He won't get this one. I'm running short myself and I won't have time to get to Ike South if we gotta drag him around." He let my head go and deliberately, I let it slump back down.

Now everything was screwed up proper. Real *snafu*. The one thing that broke me out of the big bind in the restaurant winds up in a hype's pocket and I'm worse off than I ever was.

Think, boy, I told myself. Think awfully hard. Life in colleg- those two years way back so long ago. Show your book learning. You got going against you only one scrawny doped up punk and a broad Big Stipetto kept on the side. How formidable could they be?

Pretty formidable. Before I could think Fly sung at the back of my head and that far off sound of metal on bone, quieted by a small layer of flesh in between, reached me from far off and the black was with me again.

When sense and sound and sight came back, it flushed a searing pain down the back of my skull into my spine. It lasted a few minutes before settling down to a steady throbbing at the base of my head. This time I was on the floor, my hands behind me, my ankles tied and drawn up so they touched my fingers. In the old days they used to throw a loop around your neck too so that any movement would mean you choked yourself to death.

Fly said, "He's okay now. You okay, Ryan?"

I swore at him.

"See, I told you he was all right. I don't know why the hell you was worried about him. Big Step is only gonna knock him off anyway. Now you wait here and don't leave, you hear?"

"I'm not staying . . ."

"Maybe you'd like for me to pass that on to Big Step. He'd flatten your face agin, you give him any trouble now. Maybe nobody'll come in, but if'n they do, somebody better be here to steer 'em off."

"You hurry," Lisa sulked.

"Nuts, baby. Nobody's hurryin' Big Step. First I gotta find him. He ain't gonna be a happy one when I do. With Little Step dead he's liable to come over here running. Maybe he'll want to wait to enjoy what he's gonna do even more. You just stay put."

Fly left without saying anything further. I lay there staring at the dark, until the line of light that marked the door suddenly blossomed and the switch clicked the room into a bright, painful glare.

Lisa said, "You're sure a trouble maker, Ryan."

A long time ago Lisa Williams has been a beautiful doll. She had soloed at the Copa, done two musicals on Broadway and seemed headed for Hollywood. She was still beautiful in one way. There weren't many girls who were built like her. She was one full breasted, heavy-thighed bundle of sex that was a marvel to look at. Then you reached her face. Something had happened to it. A car accident could have done it. So could a pair of brutal fists. Big Primo Stipetto didn't like his sex machines playing around in other back yards. In his own with his kid brother Penny, it was even worse.

I said, "Hello, Lisa. It's been pretty long."

"Hasn't it though." She paused, looked quickly at her hands, then said absently, "What'd you want to get messed up with Big Step for?"

"I didn't know I was."

"He's real old fashioned, Ryan. Anyone who touches his kid brother goes face to face with him. You shouldn't 've killed the kid."

"Look . . . I didn't kill the kid."

"Oh Ryan . . ."

I sucked my breath in, held it and shook my head to clear it. "Penny Stipetto was a cinch to get bumped one day. So he came after me and if he had tried it I would have taken him apart. Somebody else did it, though. Not me."

"Ryan . . . I . . ."

"Forget it, kid."

She watched me a moment, biting her lower lip between her teeth. "I can't forget it. I remember . . . other things."

"Well don't then."

"That's not easy to do."

"Give it a hard try."

"Don't be so damn tough, Irish. Maybe I just don't like to be in somebody's debt. Ever think of it that way? Just because you kept that crazy Doe Wenzel from shooting me and took the slug yourself . . . oh, hell."

"Listen," I told her, "forget the bit. You don't owe me anything."

A cramp caught at the muscles in my lower back and I arched against the ropes. I could feel the tendons pull taut from my neck down and for a full minute the paralyzing agony of the thing held me rigid.

Before I could stop her she was on her knees crying softly, her fingers tearing at the knots on the rope and then suddenly I was free to move and the relief of it was almost too much to take. I lay there and tried to come back to normal slowly and when I made it I said, "Thanks."

"Who was I fooling anyway," Lisa said.

We both heard the door slam out front at the same time. I waved her out quickly, shut the door and put my ear to it. Fly came back in the other room, breathing hard, his voice tight with excitement. "I got Big Step right off on the phone. By damn, he's coming over now. You hear that . . . *now*. We'll have a real party, by damn.

That wise punk'll get his good for sure now. We're gonna do it right here in about five minutes. Boy, I'm gonna enjoy tellin' that punk!"

His feet came across the room, he yanked the door open and there I stood, grinning at him. It took a good three seconds before his hopped up mind realized the full implications of what he was seeing, then before he could move I chopped one across his jaw to shut him down. I put too much mad behind it. He was too small and I was too big for so much mad. He half flew back across the room, skidding on his back, then rolled once and lay in a soft heap with blood running down his chin and his breath dragging in through a twisted jaw.

I found my .45 in his waistband, then probed through his pockets for the capsule. When I didn't find it I tried the seams, the linings, his shoes and every place he could have had it on him. But it wasn't there.

Lisa said suddenly, "Ryan . . . Big Step . . ."

I nodded. "Yeah. Five minutes." I had maybe two left. I couldn't afford to take the chance on staying. I got up, looked at her squarely and said, "He took a cap off me. I need it." When her eyes went funny I added, "I'm not on the stuff. There was something else in that cap besides H."

"I'll . . . I'll try," she said hesitantly.

"Okay baby. And thanks again. Just tell Primo Stippetto Fly did a lousy job tying me up. Now hold still a second."

She saw what I was going to do and never moved. I hit her just right so there would be no doubt about what happened when Big Step came in. I put her down easy and got out of there.

* * *

I got word to Pete-the-Dog to meet me at Tony Bay's deli and he left his news stand long enough to fake picking up a sandwich. It was a smart move because Pete told me both Newbolder and Schmidt had been alternating holding a steady stakeout on my apartment and detailed a guy new to plainclothes to watch him and a few others on the block. Homicide had a blanket over the area and I was to be the pigeon.

Pete said, "You're nuts to move around daytimes, Ryan."

"I got no choice, kid. Look you hear any word about Penny Stipetto?"

"Word? Man, that's all I hear. You're their boy, you know that."

"But you know better."

"Sure," Pete nodded, "I do, but I ain't Big Step. After the other brother catching it he's laying it all on you. I'm hearing thing's would scare a snake."

"I got a favor coming, Pete?"

"Anytime. Just anytime."

"Start asking. Somebody around must've seen something when Penny got it."

"In this town two blocks away is somebody else's turf, Irish. Over there they're more scared of the Stipettos than they like you. These days it's real nervous."

"So ask around. Don't stick your neck out, but see what you can pick up."

"Okay, I can do that. Who you want off your neck first, the fuzz or Step?"

I grinned at him, just a little guy, a nobody with a paper stand, but a heart as big as your hat and ready to do anything for a friend he was asked to.

"Any help in either direction will be fine," I told him.

He let out a low chuckle and picked up his wrapped sandwich. "Boy, your connections sure went sour fast. I thought you had an in with the fuzz after that job last year. I thought you was some kind of hero."

"Nobody's nothing with the murder squad when they

23

think you pulled a big hit. They gave me one break. They won't give me two."

"Tough. Anything you want from the house?"

"No. I can get in if I want to. Better if I stayed away though. If you pick up anything, call me at Andy's."

"Right."

I plucked a late copy of the paper from his pocket. "This mine?"

Pete-the-Dog nodded, grinned and walked away. I took the paper out the back door with barely a nod at Tony Bay and opened it up in the alley.

My publicity was a full page wide.

In brief, it stated that in an attempt to apprehend a suspected killer, a gunfight ensued with the wanted man's confederates during which time four persons were killed and several injured. Among the dead were Vincent (Little Step) Stipetto, Carl Hoover and Moe Green, associates of the notorious Primo (Big Step) Stipetto. The other dead man was identified as one Lewis Coyne, address unknown. Two other men engaged in the gunfight escaped, as did "Irish" Ryan, the one suspected of having gunned down Fred (Penny) Stipetto.

For a street shooting of that size, the account was awfully vague. I was suspected of being a target for the Stipettos, yet accused of having them on my side, their diversionary shooting getting me off the hook. Nobody seemed to have pieced the thing together and if they had, it wasn't given to the reporters.

Karen Sinclair was listed as critically wounded and taken to Bellevue Hospital and identified as a secretary in the FCC offices in Manhattan, but that was all.

And I was in the middle of a real fine mess. Like before, everybody wants to kill me and while they try I'm supposed to deliver a lost state secret to somebody who will nab me if I do.

24

Great life for a hood.

From a luncheonette near Seventh I called the hospital. I gave a phony name, said I was an AP correspondent and queried the operator about the condition of Karen Sinclair. Habit got the better of her and she put me through to the floor. Someone told me Karen Sinclair was still on the critical list and not available for an interview. I thanked them and hung up. I changed phones before making the next call, figuring that if the Sinclair dame had been telling the truth, there'd be Federal fuzz running down every lead they got.

The operator at the precinct house switched me into the office and a heavy voice said, "Newbolder speaking."

"This is Ryan, Sergeant."

After a moment's heavy pause Newbolder said in a bored tone, "All right, boy, where are you?"

"Public phone. Don't bother tracing it. I'll be out of here in a minute."

He knew it and I could tell he wasn't going to be bothered trying. Maybe he was still remembering last year. "Are you coming in?"

"Not yet. I have something I have to do first."

"Oh?" His voice was too soft.

"Let's get something straight first. Don't waste time trying to hang Penny Stipetto's killing on me. I didn't pull it off. I had nothing at all to do with that hit. You poke around for another angle and you'll get some answers."

He didn't answer me at first, then he said quietly, "I didn't think you did. You looked good for it though. Besides, you'd be better off in custody than having Big Step breathing down your throat."

"He doesn't bother me."

"No? Well he bothers me now. He's ready to blow the top off things."

"Let him. What about the Sinclair girl?"

25

Newbolder came back too fast. "What about her?"

"She talk?"

He still spoke too fast. "What would she have to say?"

"That's what I'm wondering."

"Damn you, Ryan . . ."

"She's in the picture, Sergeant. That mess last night wasn't all me. Big Step had his men out there waiting for me, but she was something right out of the blue."

"Ryan . . ." I knew he was signalling for a tracer now and cursing himself for not having put one on the phone before.

I said, "I'll call you back, kiddo," and hung up.

Now the bit was tighter than ever.

Until now Newbolder had figured that the Sinclair dame sitting with me was a pure accident and I took advantage of the diversion she stirred up outside to take off. Now he was figuring me as being part of a larger picture. In a way it was good. I could always get the fuzz for company real fast if I needed them.

Chapter 3

The day man at the Woolsey-Lever Hotel was Lennie
Ames and he owed me a favor. Two years ago he had
been making book right at the desk when a team from
vice came in to tag him, only I spotted them first,
picked up his briefcase of receipts, markers and cash and
walked off with the evidence. He got them back after
the heat was off and never had the nerve to get in the
game again. And I hadn't asked for the favor back until
now.

When I walked into the shabby, off-Broadway hotel,
Lennie Ames spotted me coming through the door and
turned white. Like everybody else, he had seen the
papers, only he knew what was coming up. With the
barest nod of his head he motioned toward the office and
I went in, shut the door and waited. Two minutes later
Lennie came in quickly, eased the door closed and
plunked down in his chair behind the desk. "Irish . . .
for Pete's sake . . ."

Before he could finish I said, "I'm collecting now,
buddy."

"Does it have to be me? Man, ever since those hustlers
got rousted off Eighth they've been operating out of
here. Every night some plainclothes dick comes prowling
around. Yesterday there's an investigator from the
D.A.'s office in asking questions . . ."

"All I want is a room and no trouble."

"You already got the trouble."

"That's something I have to clean up."

He got up, walked to the window and peered out
through the venetian blinds, then closed them all the

way. "Look, Ryan, the cops I can steer off, but suppose that Stipetto mob tracks you here? You think they won't put things together? They know what you did one time. So they'll squeeze me and I squeeze easy. I'm chicken, man. I'm ready to run right now. Big Step will put a slug in me as fast as he will you if he knows I'm hiding you out."

"I don't remember waiting to be asked to do a favor that last time, Lennie."

He looked at me, his eyes mirroring his embarrassment. "Okay, Irish, so I was a heel for a while." He grinned at me and tried to light a cigarette with hands that shook enough so that it took two matches to do it. "We keep a spare on the fourth floor northwest corner. It's marked MAINTENANCE SUPPLIES and has an exterior fire escape exit that leads down to the courtyard in back. There's a john, a wash basin and a cot in there and you don't have to register. The handyman who used it died in a sanatarium three months ago and we've been contracting our maintenance work, such as it is. Any questions, you tell them you and he made the arrangements. Leave me out of it."

"Good enough. What about the night manager?"

"A screaming fag afraid of his own shadow. He's had a lot of trouble and we're the only ones who'll give him a job. He'll do anything to keep it. I'll take care of him."

"You'll tell him then?"

"Damn right. It's better they know. I'll tell him you'll land on him like a ton of bricks if he opens his mouth." Lennie pulled the drawer out, threw me a key and said, "It's all yours now. Don't do me any more favors and I won't do you any."

"Sure," I said, pocketed the key and left.

It was only a little cubicle, but it was enough. I could sweat out the days there and use the phone if I had to. The door had a barrel bolt on the inside and the window went up easily. I cased the yard, spotted a handy exit through the six foot fences if I needed it, then flopped down on the cot.

Now was a time for thinking.

I had walked into one hell of a mess. Big Step thought I knocked off his brother and I had the motive, the ability and the time to do it. So he was after me.

The fuzz took the same attitude on recommendation from their varied sources of information and were scouring the city for me. I had a record of arrests even if there were no convictions and they'd love to see me take a fall. I had been in their hair too damn long.

Karen Sinclair was next. If she told me straight, and there was no reason for her not to, I was right in the middle of somebody else's game. She claimed to be a Federal agent and nobody was saying anything. Her job with the FCC could be a great cover. She had passed me something that could make or break our national security and I boffed it.

Damn it, I felt like one hungry trout in a small pond on the opening day of the fishing season! A lousy rabbit that accidentally jumped the fence into a pen of starving hounds.

First move then: I could clean Big Step off my back and the fuzz too if I found Penny Stipetto's killer. But that left Karen Sinclair and the ones she spotted tailing her. That left a whole damn Federal agen y who would be breathing down my throat for that capsule.

And Fly had that.

So find Fly first. Go into Big Step's back yard and find Fly. It wasn't going to be easy. The little weasel never holed up in the same place twice and slept in as many doorways as he did beds, but he did leave himself wide open on one count . . . he had told Lisa he was hurting for a blast and thought the cap he took from me was heroin.

If it was, there could be trouble. If it wasn't, the trouble was even worse. I had to find out.

Dusk came a little after seven and as soon as the supper crowd had cleared the streets I went back downstairs, got a scared glance from the gay boy at the desk and went outside to the drugstore on the corner and put in a call to Bill Grady who did a syndicated column across the nation and waited for him to answer.

His secretary asked me who I was and I gave the name of the State Senator. It got action fast. She told me he was at his hotel, gave me the number to call and before she could notify him I had my dime in the slot and was dialing.

I said, "Grady?"

"Roger. Who's this?"

"Irish."

There was silence for a second, then: "Boy, you sure don't fool around. Where are you?"

"Not too far away. Can we talk?"

"Come on up."

"There's a statute about aiding and abetting."

"So I've heard. There's also freedom of the press and the unwritten law of protecting news sources. I smell a story."

"Ten minutes."

"I'll be waiting. Alone."

Bill Grady lived in a hotel on West Seventy-Second Street, an old conservative place left over from a different era. I took the elevator up to his floor, touched the buzzer and when he opened the door, stepped inside. I hadn't seen him for three years, but it didn't make any difference. We were still a couple of Army buddies who had a short lifetime together and nothing had changed.

We had one drink before he nodded to a chair and said, "Sit down and talk. You're the hottest item in town."

I shook my head. "It only looks that way, friend."

"Oh?"

"Are we off the record?"

"Natch. Shoot."

So I told him. When I finished he still hadn't touched his drink, but his face looked tight and his fingers were bloodless around the glass in his hand. I said, "What's the matter?"

He took a sip of his highball and put the glass down. "You've just confirmed something that's been a rumor if I read it right."

"So tell me."

Grady hesitated, debating within himself what he should let out. Finally he turned around and stared at me. "I trusted you with my life a few times. I don't see why you'd blow the whistle on this. Have you read about the Soviet oceanography work going on since '46?"

"Some. They've been mapping the ocean floor, studying currents, tidal effects, marine life and all that jazz. Why?"

"You know how the Polaris missile works, don't you?"

"Compressed air fired from a submerged vessel until airborne then rocket effect takes over with a guidance system to the target. Where does that come in?"

"The Reds have been working in International waters about twenty miles off our coasts for years. There's nothing we can do about it except keep them under surveillance. Supposing they developed a Polaris-type missile and located them on a permanent pad a few miles from our shorelines. A half dozen could destroy our major seaport cities, population and military bases with one touch of a button. They could sit there unde-tected until they were ready to be used and then we'd have it."

"You said they were under surveillance."

"Irish buddy, the ocean is a big place. Submarine

31

development and underwater exploration has come a long way. They could have had decoys going while the real thing sneaked up past our screen and while we're tangled in nuclear disarmament talks and peace treaties, playing big brother to all the slobs in the world, the Soviets are laying the groundwork for our own destruction if the surface negotiations don't go their way. Like idiots, our military appropriations don't allow for full protection. The jerks who handle the loot fight a war in Viet Nam with WWII aircraft, let our guys get killed, they yank out MacArthur who could have won the Korean thing, they make us look stupid around the globe and dig their own graves while they all try to soak up newspaper space so they can run for office when they get promoted up and out."

"Get to the point."

Bill Grady nodded and made himself another drink. He swirled the ice around in the glass and took a swallow from it. "From unauthorized sources, I hear Karen Sinclair was a Fed, all right. I checked her b.g. and she was an Oceanography major at a west coast university. She started out on an assignment with six others, all of whom have died under peculiar circumstances. A further check puts her with a relatively unimportant Navy department engaged in subsurface research, ostensibly charting the shelf off our coast. Let's suppose her job was a secret one, to locate these possible underwater missile sites. Let's suppose she did. You think the Soviets wouldn't be aware of their presence and try to stop it? But let's suppose she alone got away with a record of their positions somehow. They couldn't afford to let her live. She couldn't be left to make her contact. They would have put every resource at their command to nail her and it looks like they might have . . . and you, my friend, were entrusted with the goodies."

I got up, my lips tight across my mouth. "Why me?"

"Because she had to do something and you look like you do."

"Nuts!" I slammed the drink down and glared at him. "That's too damn many suppositions. I don't like any of them."

Quietly, he said, "Suppose they're true?"

"Why the hell do I have to get trapped in the middle?"

"Kismet, my friend. Maybe you're lucky." He took a pull of the drink again. "Or maybe all of us are." Then he looked at me and waited.

"All right, Grady, cut it fine. If I go to the cops they slap my can in a cell for homicide. I sweat. If I tap the Feds they turn me over to the cops anyway. If I give them the story they won't believe me because I can't come up with a lousy capsule and Karen Sinclair isn't able to talk. If she dies, I'll be dead too. If I prowl the streets, either Big Step hits me or the cops do, so where does that leave me?"

For the first time Bill Grady let out a sardonic laugh. "I don't know, old buddy, but it's going to be mighty interesting. Even your obituary written from a speculative viewpoint ought to buy new readers."

"Great. Thanks a bunch."

"No trouble."

"And where do you go from here?"

His grin got bigger. "Nowhere. I'm going to sit back and watch. I want to see a big war hero who digs the hood bit turn patriotic, not because he wants to, but because he has to. It will be an interesting study in human behavior. You've always been an enigma to everybody, now here's your chance to be an even bigger one. All I want is the story."

"Go screw yourself."

"Physically impossible," he laughed again. "It's you who's screwed. To make it worse I went and upset your weird idea of morality and now I want to see the action.

You got no choice any longer, Irish. You're the only one who knows all the facts you have to get out of the trap. If you do and when you do, I'll rate a scoop bonus. How about that?"

I put my glass down and stood up. "Maybe, Bill, maybe."

"What's with the maybe?"

"I might need a liaison man. If you want the story, then you're tagged." He licked his lips, slammed one hand into the other and said, "I might have figured it. So what do you want?"

"Get me in to see Karen Sinclair."

"It can't be done. You'll be spotted. She's got a uniformed police guard and a dozen of the pretty boys stationed around her room. It's impossible."

"So do it anyway," I told him.

*   *   *

At ten p.m. a makeup man from NBC dropped a curly headed rug over my short hair, fitted me with a London mustache, clear-lensed glasses and with a Graflex in my hand, I passed for a Manchester newspaperman whose press card had been lifted from a passed-out owner an hour before. We both had to put down a gallon of ginger ale before he went out on double scotches, but it worked and we made the front desk where a police spokesman told us Karen Sinclair was still too critical to be interviewed. A group of other reporters gave us the laugh for making the try and went back to playing cards on an upside down tray set on their knees.

But Grady didn't stop there. He got the plainclothes man down in the lobby. "Look, maybe she can't talk, but all we want to do is make sure."

The cop said, "Sorry, she isn't to be seen."

"Maybe there's more here than we know about. Since when do innocent bystanders in a shooting get this kind of treatment? I think a little legwork might come up with a tasty bit."

The young guy in the blue gabardine frowned. "Listen . . . "

"I don't listen to anybody. I write, mister. I do a column and have *carte blanche* and if you want it that way, I can raise a lot of interesting questions."

"Wait here a minute," the guy said. He walked to a phone, dialed a number and spoke for a good two minutes. When he came back he nodded for us to follow him. "You can take a look . . . that's all. She's out cold and there's nothing more to it than that. She has a police guard because of this Stipetto business and she might have been a possible eye witness to what happened."

I picked it up quicker than Grady did. "What do you mean . . . what happened?"

The guy was trapped. All he could do was say, "Sorry but . . . "

Before he could turn away I grabbed his arm. "You mean there was more than the shooting?"

When he turned around he was composed again, his face inscrutable. "If you're a police reporter you know what I mean about eye witnesses. Now if you want to see the dame, you have one minute to take a look."

"Sure, but you know us," I said. "Always questions."

"Yeah, but keep it quiet. You'll be the first ones allowed in for a look, and no pictures," he added, pointing to my camera.

I acknowledged and slapped the Graflex shut. The elevator took us to the sixth floor where our guide led us past the others stationed at strategic points along the corridor. The doctor met us at the door, told us to be quick and make no noise, then turned the knob, spoke to the nurse inside and let us pass.

Somebody had taken off Karen Sinclair's makeup and for the first time, I saw her as she was. Even lying there, her face waxen pale, she was a stunning woman, the sheets adhering to every contour of that magnificent body, the lustrous gleam of her chestnut hair framing her beauty. One shoulder was swathed in bandages and another was outlined at her waist.

The nurse beside us reached for her pulse automatically, seemed satisfied and laid her arm back down. "How badly was she shot?" I asked her.

"Luckily, clean wounds. The bullets missed vital organs."

"Is she out of danger?"

"That is for the doctor to say. Now if you don't mind . . ." She walked to the door and held it open. Grady followed her, but I hesitated just a moment. There was a barely perceptible flicker of her eyelids, then they opened slightly and she was looking at me.

I had to do it quickly. I had to make myself known and hope she could think fast despite her condition. I knew I was unrecognizable by my face, but I could duplicate a situation. Without moving my lips, I said softly, "What was the powder in the capsule? Was it heroin?"

For a half second there was no response, then she got it. In the same way, with no motion, her voice a whisper, she said, "Powdered sugar." Then her eyes closed again and I walked away.

Our impatient guide who waited for us in the corridor said, "Satisfied?"

Bill nodded and shrugged. "Sorry to bother you. It's nice to be sure."

"The press will be officially notified of any changes.

We'd appreciate it if you would not speculate and stay with the communiques."

"Sure." Bill looked at me. "Let's go. Thanks for the tour."

The guy bobbed his head. "Don't mention it . . . to the other reporters, I mean."

When we were on the steps outside the hospital, I steered Grady to one side and held a match up to the cigarette in his mouth. "They have something hot on this one. Did you get what he said in the beginning?"

"About what happened?"

"Yeah."

"Let's make a phone call. I have a solid in at headquarters. They'll feed me any action if I promise not to let it out until it's cleared."

We crossed the street to a drug store and I waited while Bill put in his call. When he came out of the booth his face was serious, his eyes dark with concern. He sucked nervously on the cigarette and let the smoke stream through his nostrils. "Well?"

"You could have been the key, Irish," he told me. "She was an agent, all right."

"That wasn't what you had on your mind."

He dropped the butt and ground it out under his heel. "The police recovered the spent slugs and matched them with the guns. The shots that hit her didn't come from the police or Stipetto guns. Bullets from those guns got Vincent Stipetto and Moe Green too." He looked at me hard. "Can you break it down now?"

"I think so," I said, "The Stipetto mob was laying for me. When she came out the others starting banging away and the Stipetto boys were caught in between and thought it was part of a crash out on my part. They never lived long enough to find out different. Then Newbolder and Schmidt made the scene and nailed the rest of the gang. In the meantime, the others saw Karen

37

go down and since they thought they nailed their target, they cut out. All the cops saw was the Stipetto boys, tied them in with me and didn't look any further."

"Until now," he mused.

"And where do they go from here?"

"No place until the Sinclair woman can talk. She's the crux. She brought the thing to a head. Trouble is, none of it's over. She's still alive and you're still free."

"And you got my obituary already written."

"No," Bill said, "but I'm thinking of it."

Chapter 4

Through Pete-the-Dog I passed the word down the street to start scratching for Fly. He was hooked on H and someplace he had to locate a source of supply so he'd be hitting a dealer. If he tried mainlining with the sugar in the capsule he'd find out in a hurry he had nothing going for him and would do a crazy dance to get a charge. He wouldn't even try to be careful and the word would go out like a brush fire. What I had to hope for was that he wouldn't discard the microfilm in the capsule where I couldn't find it. A junkie with a big hurt liable to do anything. If I was lucky he'd keep the cap for a reserve and stick with his regular pusher. He had been in the business long enough to have solid contacts but let trouble touch a hophead and everybody steered clear. Right now little old Fly could have trouble if I knew Big Step. For letting me bust loose he could be getting the hard squeeze.

Chuck Vinson's saloon had a side entrance and I didn't have to go through the bar to snag a booth in the back room. I took the furthest one back and pushed the button for the waiter. Old Happy Jenkins came shuffling back napkin over one arm and a bowl of pretzels in his hand. He had to peer at me over his glasses a second before he saw who it was, then he swallowed hard and looked back toward the front with eyes suddenly scared.

"You bugs, Irish? You outa your mind? What the hell you doon in here?"

"Trying to get a beer," I said.

"A half hour ago Big Step himself come in asking.

Chuck said he ain't seen you but it don't mean they ain't covering from outside."

"So I'm all shook up over it. Do I get that beer?"

"Irish . . . come on. Step had that new guy with him—the one from Miami. They're looking, man. They want you bad."

"Doesn't everybody?"

He licked his lips again and edged in closer. "The cops got a tail on Step in case he finds you. You know that too?"

"It figures. Now get me a tall Piel's with a foamy head like you see on TV and I'll blow. And ask Chuck if I got any phone calls."

Happy nodded joylessly and shuffled off. Two minutes later he was back with a Stein, slid it over in front of me and said, "You got a call from somebody." He handed me a matchbook cover with a number scrawled on it. "You gotta buzz 'em back Chuck says not to use his place like an office while the heat's on."

When he left I finished half the beer, found a dime and hopped into the phone booth beside me. The number was a Trafalgar exchange which put it somewhere in the West Seventies but I didn't recognize it. The phone rang just once before it was picked up and a cautious voice said, "Yeah?"

"Irish. You call?"

"Where you at?"

"Chuck Vinson's."

That seemed to satisfy him. He said, "Pete-the-Dog saw me today. Said you wanted to know about Fly."

"Got anything?"

"No, but I know where he gets his junk from. He was peddling for Ernie. Ernie paid him off in H. If you want Fly, try him."

"Thanks buddy. What do I owe you?"

"Nothin'. You took me out of a jam once. We're

40

square now" He hung up abruptly and I stood there for a minute trying to figure out who it was. Hell, a lot of people owed me favors. I went back, finished my beer and went out the same way I came in, mixing with a group going past the door to the subway station.

Ernie South had started off in the wholesale candy business fifteen years ago, working the fringe areas of Harlem before he switched to dope. He had peddled the stuff for Treetop Coulter before he took his first fall, did his time in Sing Sing, then came back and muscled Treetop right out of the business. He wound up operating in Big Primo Stipetto's territory, managed to get himself in the good graces of the boss and ran a neat operation the cops weren't able to break.

Everybody had been hearing a lot about Ernie South lately. He and Penny Stipetto were thick as blood brothers, especially since '62 when Big Step turned over a prime section uptown to his kid brother to run as he saw fit. Penny Stipetto had been on the verge of being a big time operator when he was knocked off and since they thought I was his killer, Ernie South would have his hands out looking for me too. Penny's death left the section wide open and until Big Step moved back in or designated another lieutenant to handle it, Ernie was moving things around.

Damn it! I should have kept my hands to myself, but when Penny tore into old Rudy Max and broke him up for not paying protection money to operate a newsstand I couldn't help myself. I broke his jaw and four ribs and left him in a mess of his own blood on the side walk, not giving a damn how big he or his brothers were. Two of his men were right there when it happened and neither of them had the guts to go for a rod because they knew I had a blaster in my belt and would chop them down the second they moved. They had seen it happen before. No, they could wait. Big brother Step would take care of

41

it if Penny didn't. Only Penny Stipetto didn't want to look like a lily with everybody waiting to see how he took it. No, he had to go gunning for me himself.

And somebody else nailed him.

Why?

It didn't take too much doing to locate Ernie South. I had enough friends in the area who didn't dig the narcotics bit and had seen too much heat brought in on their own operations because of his. They were glad to pinpoint him at a sleezy gin mill that featured a belly dancer, and let me work out my own arrangements with him. They knew damn well there was a price on my head from all directions, but they had lived under the shakedown racket Big Step ran too long to help him out any. All I got was a word to watch myself, a couple offers of an assist I waved off and a silent word that meant they hoped I could make something stick.

For an hour and a half I stood across the street waiting, watching the customers come and go until the place was almost empty. Then, through the window, I saw Ernie flip a bill to the bartender, say something they both thought was funny, then go to the door.

He was looking west watching for a cab when I put the nose of the .45 in his ribs and said, "Hello, Ernie."

Even before he turned around he started to shake like he was going to come apart at the seams. He stiffened, seemed to rise on his toes and twisted just enough to see me. Then his eyes met mine briefly and a smile flickered across his mouth and he relaxed until he was almost casual. "You're taking big chances these days, Irish."

"Not from you, punk." I nudged him with the gun, ran my hand over his pockets and beltline to make sure he wasn't heeled and said, "Start walking. Get out of line just once and you've had it, boy." I wasn't putting on an act. I'd scatter his guts over the street as fast as I'd look at him and he knew it, but he knew it didn't have to happen either so he simply shrugged and turned toward Broadway and strolled along with me at his side like a couple of buddies.

"You're in the wrong end of town, Irish, Big Step has his people all over the place."

"Then hope we don't meet any. You'll catch the first one."

I saw his nervous glance to both sides of the street, hoping nobody would show. Hopheads Ernie could handle. Me he couldn't. "What's the gimmick?" he asked. "We never tangled. I'm not any part of the show."

"I want Fly. He peddled around for you and you supplied his H. Where is he?"

"How the hell should I know?"

"The last time I saw him he needed to blast bad. You're his source."

Ernie South didn't answer me. He reached for a cigarette and lit it with a hand that shook badly.

I said, "Ernie, I'm going to point this rod at your leg. I'm going to put one right through the back of your knee and roll out of here before a squad car can get near the place. You'll be going around on an aluminium and plastic peg the rest of your life."

He tried to sound calm about it. "You wouldn't do it."

"Remember Junior Swan? Ever see his hands? He can't use either of them now. Remember Buck Harris and Sy Green? Sy's mind is going on him now and Buck is still in a wheelchair in a charity ward trying to forget that night."

Ernie remembered all right. I could see the sweat on his forehead glistening under his hatbrim. He swallowed, wiped his hand across his face and half whispered, "So Fly's on the *out* list. He don't get a thing from nobody."

"Why?"

43

"Because Big Step said so. He's making Fly hurt for doing a dumb thing like he did with you."

"Where is he, Ernie?"

"I don't know! I . . ."

He heard the .45 go off half cock and the tiny click was like a sonic boom in his ears. "Come on, Irish, I don't know where he is. Try somebody else!"

"Name them."

"Cortez maybe. Connie Morse or Joey Gomp on Ninety-Sixth Street. He used to hit them sometimes."

"That's still Big Step's territory."

"Sure, and they're all cuttin' him off. So try downtown. He had some contacts there only don't ask who. My turf is here. I don't know them guys."

I knew he was telling the truth. Ernie South wasn't about to lie to me right ther or he knew what would happen. "Where's his pad, Ernie?"

"Basement joint two places down from Steve's Diner on Second."

I caught the expression that came into his face and let him feel a touch of the gun again. "Finish it, Ernie."

He was caught and knew it. If he didn't lay it on the line he knew I'd come looking for him. He said, "Big Step's got a man covering the place."

"Why?"

"So Fly can't make his pad if he's got anything stashed away in there."

"Nice. Step holds a big mad, doesn't he?"

"You'll find out," he said viciously.

"Who killed Penny Stipetto, Ernie?"

He stopped then, turned his head to look directly at me and his eyes were black with hate. His whole face seemed drawn in a tight mask. I grinned at him deliberately and shook my head. "Not me, boy."

"You're dead, Ryan. You might just as well jump in front of a subway and get it over with."

I thumbed the .45 back on half cock again and shoved it under my belt. "When I go it'll be the hard way and it won't be alone. Go tell Big Step I'm looking for him."

He almost ran getting to the corner and when he was out of sight I cut across the street, through an alley and came out the other side, flagged down a cab and told him to take me to the Cafeteria. Big Step, Newbolder, Schmidt and the rest might be looking for me but they wouldn't be expecting me to turn up in a place I ate in five nights a week. Enough of the Broadway crowd would be on hand as usual to pass me any information if they weren't too scared of the action.

Wally Pee was the first one to spot me and he almost spilled his coffee. He gave me the signal that he was no good for talking and let his eyes sidle to the back corner where Izzy Goldwitz was finishing a pot pie with his usual relish. I walked up, got a cup of coffee and took it back to Izzy's table where I sat down with my back to the rest. It could be a fatal mistake, but I didn't want anybody picking up by sight. Izzy got that sick look again and couldn't finish his pot pie, reaching for his coffee to quiet down what was happening to his stomach.

When he put the cup down his eyes pleaded with me. "Get lost, Irish. Get away from me, huh? You got this town on its ear already and I don't want to be there when the shooting starts again."

"No sweat, Izzy. All I want is Fly. You see him around?"

"Me, I don't see nothing. Now scram, okay?"

"Fly's hitting all the suppliers."

"I know. Big Step's got him cut off. Fly's taking a cure whether he likes it or not and it'll kill him for letting you off the hook. So whatta you want him for? Another guy was looking for him before. Got Pedro the bus boy all shook"

I frowned at him. "Who?"

"I dunno. Ask Pedro. Just get away from me."

"Sure, Izzy. Thanks."

"From you I want nothin', not even thanks."

Pedro was a little Puerto Rican with a multiplicity of last names nobody could pronounce who worked his heart out hustling dirty dishes to support six brothers and sisters. He was quick as a banty rooster and always ready with a big smile, but when I found him in the back room off the kitchen he was neither quick nor smiling. He was sitting on an upturned lard bucket, his head in his hands and when I came in he jumped, his face contorted, his hands clutching his belly.

I said, "Hi, Pete."

When he recognized me he tied on a smile but it didn't fit very well and he dropped it. "Mr. Ryan," he acknowledged softly.

"What happened, kid?"

"I theenk nothing happened, please."

With my toe I hooked an empty coke box and set it up so I could squat down beside him. "Let's have it Pete. Who took you apart?"

"It ees nothing."

"Don't kid me. I'll find out anyway, so save yourself some grief. Whoever did it can come back."

Sudden terror filled his eyes and he huddled up against the wall, his teeth biting into his lip. He looked at me, shrugged resignedly. "A man, he look for Fly. He look for you too."

"Who came first?"

"You, Mr. Ryan. He ask about you the other night. I theenk he is police and I tell heem how you left here. I tell heem how Fly was back there waiting too."

"What else?"

"Nothing. I can't tell heem where you are. I tell heem where Fly lives after he hit me."

"Describe him."

46

"Not beeg as you, Mr. Ryan. Funny voice like I have to speak English, only different. Very bad man. Mad."

"So you know where Fly is?"

He shook his head. "No. I do not see him seence then."

"He was your friend, Pete. You know he was hooked on H?"

"Sure, I know."

"Do you know where he gets his stuff?"

"Before, from Ernie South mostly. Now, I do not know."

"Anybody around here?"

"Nobody will sell to Fly now. He ees in a very bad way, I theenk."

I stood up and rubbed the top of his head. "Okay, kid, thanks. Don't you worry about the guy coming back. Until it's over you'll get a little cover."

"Please, you don't have to . . ."

"No sweat, Pete. No trouble at all." I grinned at him and this time he managed a small smile for real. I said, "There a phone around here?"

He pointed toward the door. "Right inside the kitchen."

I reached Newbolder at his home after the precinct gave me his number. He said, "Sergeant Newbolder speaking, who is this?"

"Your buddy, Irish."

He didn't say anything for a few seconds and I could hear him breathing, then flick on a cigarette lighter. "Okay, I can't put a tracer on your call from here, Irish. Now what's the pitch?"

"There's a kid at the Cafeteria, a bus boy named Pedro. Maybe you'd better keep him covered for a few days. He just took a shellacking from an unknown person that might fit into your case."

I could hear a pencil scratching, then: "You got friends of your own who could do that, Ryan."

"Yeah, I know, but that's what you're for."

"Don't get snotty," he said. "You're after something."

"A hophead named Fly."

"What about him?"

"Has he been seen around?"

"No squawks on him."

"Then you'd better run him down quick before you have a corpse on your hands. Big Step cut off his supply and if he doesn't fold he'll knock off somebody to get a charge."

"Where does he fit in?"

"I'd like to tell you, copper, but if I want out of this mess I have to get out myself."

"You're not doing too well. If you make another day on the streets your luck is running first class."

"I'll play along with it."

"When you get smart, pass it up. Right now that Federal agency you shilled for a couple years ago is breathing down your neck. You're on everybody's 'S' list and it's only a matter of time. Until Big Step moves we can't lay a hand on him and by then it'll be too late, you'll be dead, so I recommend protective custody."

"And a murder charge for bumping Penny Step? No dice, Sarge."

Casually, he said, "Have it your way, friend."

"I will." Then I added, "By the way, how is Karen Sinclair?"

And just as offhandedly he said, "I couldn't tell you. An hour ago she was kidnapped from her room."

It was like I had been sapped again. "What?"

"Blame yourself a little, Irish. Try this one on your conscience if you have any."

My fingers squeezed the phone so hard my knuckles turned white. "How was it worked?"

"Two doctors under a gun. The third guy posed as an intern. He shot the guy he took the uniform from in front of the doctors and they had no choice except to go along. They moved her into an ambulance under the guard's noses and got her out. We found the ambulance ten minutes ago, but she could be anywhere by now."

"Damn!"

"So chalk one dead girl up on your list, hood. I think you got the picture pretty well by now. We took Bill Grady in and he had to lay it out for us. You've made everybody a lot of trouble and when you dream, think of that lovely broad stretched out on a slab somewhere."

Under my breath I began swearing, then stopped when I was so tight I wanted to tear the damn phone right off the wall. "They won't kill her," I said.

"No? Why?"

"Because I have what they want and it won't do them a bit of good to bump her unless they know where she dropped the little goodie they're all after."

I hung up then, stared at the phone a minute, then crossed the kitchen and took the back way out through the service entrance. Fly was the key. Someplace he was roaming around carrying a bombshell of information big enough to tear apart the world. *They* knew it and I knew it, but I couldn't get to it without making myself a target for the cops, Big Step and a team of Soviet killers.

The hell I couldn't.

I was looking for a cab when the black Chevy came idling by. The light on the corner was green and in New York you don't loaf when you have the signal on your side. It was too out of character for a cab with N.Y. plates and I had played too many games the same way not to notice it.

Even before the first shot flamed from the window I was down and rolling, scrambling sideways for the cover of the trash cans at the curb and right behind me two more rocketed off the sidewalk with a brief, shrill ricochetting scream before they plastered against the wall. I had just a single look at the face turned my way that was framed in the light of the street lamp, a sharp, hawk-like face under a shock of pitch black hair with one unruly twist of it hanging down into his eyes.

The car was gone around the corner before I could get the gun out and except for a drunk who looked at me soddenly, nobody caught the action. They heard the noise though, even if most of it was contained inside the Chevvy. Two couples were dodging traffic to get across the street, but before they made it or I had to offer any explanations, I got up, dusted myself off and started away.

The drunk wiped the drool from his mouth and laughed. "Nice friends you got, mister."

"Only the best," I told him.

So now I was being stalked. Somebody figured I might come back looking for Fly, or word would get to me about somebody looking for him. I was being set up very nicely by a pack of pros and the perimiter of the jungle was getting smaller and smaller. Well, I lived here too and I wasn't going to make it easier for them.

But I wasn't really thinking of myself. I was thinking of the loveliness of Karen Sinclair, the broad who was willing to give her life for a purpose. Now *they* had her . . . and I knew why. To break her out meant a trade . . . the microfilm for her, and even then it was a rotten deal because once they had their information back, she would go under a gun too. And what 'they wanted was in the possession of a crazy junkie who wouldn't know the time of day when I found him. *If* I found him.

Chapter 5

A couple of years ago a Fed team had me picked up. It wasn't a pinch, though I would have been better off if it were. It was a cute pressure play because they wanted my peculiar services at their command since it was the only way they could handle a project. They laid my neck on the line and I had no choice about it so I played cop with them and came out of the deal a hood-type patriot and it took a long time to wash the smell of the association out of my system. My kind of people didn't go along with any kind of cops, even a recruited hood.

Now the time for returning favors was back again. The card in my wallet was worn at the edges and a few odds and ends were scribbled across the face, but the number was still legibile and I called it. Somebody was always at that office night and day and I wasn't worried about getting an answer at this hour. The phone was lifted and a voice said, "Varlie Imports, what can I do for you?"

"Try remembering me for a starter," I said.

"Yes?" The voice was puzzled.

"The name is Ryan . . . the Irish one as you used to call me."

"One moment, please." Sound diminished as he held a hand over mouthpiece and I could barely hear the hum of voices. Then the hand was taken away and the voice that spoke to me was a different one, but one I remembered well.

There was nothing friendly there. It was cold and impersonal and said, "What do you want, Ryan?"

"To see you, Shaffer. You're picking up a tab for *me*."

"Ryan . . ."

"Uh-uh. I'll do the talking. I'm in a pay station and you can't trace the call in time so don't bother. Just go to the corner of Eighth Avenue and Forty-Fifth Street and start walking north on the west side. When I'm sure you're alone I'll contact you. Twenty minutes, that's all you have." I hung up and grinned to myself. Cliff Shaffer would be there, all right. He knew what the picture was well enough.

I knew he'd make a try for a pinch anyway so I had a friend of mine who had an independent cab out in front of the car he had stationed near the corner and block its way. Before Shaffer went fifty feet I was behind him, steered him into the hotel lobby on the corner and angled to the east-west street and started him walking. I didn't have to use the gun. Shaffer never did trust me all the way and wasn't taking any chances. When he knew I had caught the play in time, he shrugged it off and played the game. He hadn't bothered wearing a rod either.

Two blocks over was an all night diner and we had coffee and sandwiches sent back to our table and I looked at him sitting there, still the same, case hardened cop he had always been, a little grayer now with a few more wrinkles at the corners of his eyes, but a guy who headed up a tight little agency assigned to special high-priority projects only.

He looked at me just as carefully and said, "You haven't changed much, Irish."

"I'm still alive."

"For how long? There's a city wide alert on you. Or maybe Big Step will reach you first."

"You left out some tourist types, old buddy."

The hand bringing the match to his cigarette stopped in midair. "You know too much, Ryan."

52

"No . . . not quite enough. I want to stay alive and you, friend, are going to help out."

"Like hell. What you did before doesn't carry any weight now. You're just another hood to me and if I can nail you for the city boys it'll be my pleasure." He glared at me and finished lighting his butt.

"Let's put Karen Sinclair in this," I said. "Let's not make me out an idiot. I didn't get asked in, I was forced in by one of your people again and I'm tired of being a pawn."

Softly, he said, "Where do you get your information from, Irish?"

"I was a college boy once, remember? I was a war hero. I'm clever."

"You're a damned hood."

"So I like it this way. I can chisel the chiselers and don't have to pay any respect to the phony politicos who run us into the ground for their own egotistical satisfaction. I don't have to go along with the sheep who cry and bleat about the way things are and can do something about it in my own way. If this was 1776 I'd be a revolutionary and tax collectors would be fair game. I could drop the enemies trying to destroy us and be a wheel. So screw it, I'm not going to be a sheep."

His icy gray eyes ran over my face and his smile was almost deadly. "Let's talk about Karen Sinclair."

"And oceanography?" I needled him. "Or would a strip of microfilm be better, one that locates all the underwater missile pads the Soviets laid off our coastline?"

With feigned calmness Shaffer folded his hands together and leaned forward on the table. "I didn't think it was possible. I didn't think coincidence could be so damn acute. We all wondered and tried to put it together and nothing would fit."

"The ones who tailed her put it together fast enough."

He ignored me completely, following his own train of thought. "So you're the one she passed it on to. She was able to say that much but couldn't make a positive identification. We knew but we weren't sure. We didn't think it could have happened like that."

"Who are they, Shaffer?"

"Where is it, Irish?"

"Who are they?" I repeated.

Shaffer let his smile stretch across his mouth, tight and nasty. "Manos Dekker. He's the head of the thing we labeled the *Freddie Project* in Argentina, the one who killed Carlos Amega in Madrid and behind the sabotage in our installations in Viet Nam."

"Now he's here," I stated.

"I'm going to tell you a story, Irish."

"Go ahead."

"They spotted our people supposedly engaged in simple coastwise oceanography. They used a limpet and blew the *Fairway II* apart, but they didn't get the motor launch in time. Karen Sinclair and Tim Reese got away with the charts they had made and Tim microfilmed them in Miami. They got him there too, but by then Karen had the film strips but couldn't deliver because they were right behind her. Somehow she made New York. It didn't do her much good because they have their agents all over and covered all routes and were waiting for her to show up. Luckily, she spotted them and took the big chance. Unluckily, it had to be you. Now where is it?"

"Get me off the hook and maybe you'll find out."

Gently, he unlaced his fingers and shook out another cigarette. "What?"

"I know where it is. I might be able to recover it. I can't do it with the cops on my neck. I can't fight a murder charge and the Stipettos at the same time."

"Sorry, Irish."

"In that case, so am I. You'll lose an agent and all she worked for."

"Damn it, Irish . . ."

"Just do it," I said, "I don't care how. You guys have the power so make things move. You did it once before when I didn't want it, so do it now when I do or I'll resurrect that deal all over again and blow it wide open in the papers."

"Patriotism, Irish."

"Don't bother naming it. I'm saving my own neck."

"How about Karen Sinclair's? You seem to have a soft tone when you say her name."

Soft? I couldn't get her out of my mind. Ever since I saw her that's all I could think about.

"Knock if off, Shaffer. Are you coming through?"

"This time I don't have the choice, do I?"

"No."

"I'm wondering about something else too," he said. "You'd like to process this so you come out clean, wouldn't you?"

I watched him and waited.

Shaffer smiled at me and I couldn't read his face at all. "I'm going to run your gun permit through for you. You're being reactivated, Ryan."

"The hell I am!"

"Then you didn't read the fine print in those papers you signed a couple years ago. The provision was there. The penalties too."

"You bastard. I'm not playing cop again."

"Like you say, Irish boy, 'The hell you ain't.' You know where to reach me. Call in. I'll get some of the heat off your back. You take care of the rest." He got up slowly, his mouth twisting in a wry smile. "Maybe it was a good thing she did pick you out of eight million people. You're just smart enough, mean enough and evil enough to do what has to be done."

55

"Listen, Shaffer . . ."

But he wouldn't. He shook his head, holding up his hand to cut me off. "We'll have our men out too. We'll scour the city for Karen Sinclair, but we know what we're up against. This isn't a ransom snatch. It was cleverly planned and executed. The ones behind it have a motivation greater than ransom with more resources at their command than the criminal element. But in their own peculiar ways they are criminals and like the old saying goes, it takes one to catch one. Good hunting, Irish. If we can supply any leads just call. You have the number. I suggest you come down and look at our mug shots."

He turned and walked out and I cursed him silently every inch of the way to the door. The slob hung me again with my own kind and was no turning back. Even getting the heat off wasn't worth it. I liked what I was and wanted to keep it that way and now I was back on the other end of the stick again.

Damn.

Shaffer had clued his office staff. They were all the clean cut type and two of them watched me go over the mug books with narrowed eyes of disapproval. On one's desk was my dossier so I knew they had all the data from the last deal. The broad at the reception desk was the only one who seemed impressed because she took a pose with her legs so I could see the flash of white thigh above her nylons under the desk and when she brought another set of photos over she bent down deliberately to give me the benefit of an unrestricted view of ample breasts that wanted to spill out of her dress. One of the guys tightened his mouth impatiently and threw three eight by ten glossies in front of my nose and waved her out of there. "Manos Dekker," he said.

They weren't studio shots. They were taken with a long range lens and blown up, but the face and all its characteristics were there. Dekker had no stamp of nationality on him, but the set to his eyes, the flaccid mouth and the slight hump in his nose marked him a killer and a man who enjoyed his work. I had seen too many with those almost imperceptible peculiarities not to recognize the breed.

I fastened him in my mind and went back to the selected photos of other agents operating in this country. Two I knew right off, but so did everybody else. In one hazy shot that was evidently an enlargement of individuals originally in a group shot, I thought I had seen another before but couldn't quite place him. The guy at my shoulder caught my hesitation and said, "taken at a Commie meeting on the Island. Not identified."

I nodded, looked through the book and closed it. "Thanks for the trouble."

"No trouble at all," I told him.

"Any contact with those persons will be reported."

"Sure. Dead or alive?"

"Don't be funny."

Lisa Williams left very little trail. She was always on call for anything Big Step needed and if he wanted to farm her out to his boys for kicks she had to go along. Ever since he destroyed her with his fists she had lived a life of fear, indelibly tied to the punk because his mark was on her and nobody else would touch her. She hustled the upper Broadway johns for side money and spent it in the gin mills, a sucker for a touch from every stray cat type with a hard luck story.

Getting to her without making contacts with any of the Stipetto mob or their stringers who would be happy to pass on the news I was in the territory wasn't easy, but like I said before, it was my city too and there weren't many back alleys or dodges I didn't know. I had to live by them the same way they did only on a bigger scale and it took a hell of a lot more doing.

I found her in the back room of a shabby brownstone at four in the morning, a lonely voice fogged out of shape by too much booze, caroling a song from a stage hit she had been in years ago. When I knocked on the door it was as if someone had lifted the arm on a record player. The quiet was almost intense, and I knew that inside she was standing there rigid, listening hard, her heart pounding with that old fear again.

At last she said, "Yes . . . yes, who is it?"

"Irish, honey, open up."

Very slowly, the door opened on a chain and she peered out at me, eyes reddened from a big bar night, her hair dishevelled, an untidy lock of it falling across her face. "Ryan?" she said tentatively. And when she made sure it was me she bit into a knuckle and shook her head mutely.

"Let me in, girl."

"No . . . please. If anybody sees you . . ."

"Nobody saw me but they might if I stand here long enough." That decided her. She closed the door, took off the chain and held it open reluctantly. I squeezed inside, shut and locked it, then walked across the room and sat on the arm of the mohair chair by the shaded window.

"Why . . . did you come here?"

"I'm looking for Fly. You know where he is?"

She opened her mouth to lie then knew I caught it and let her head fall into her hands. "Why doesn't Big Step let him alone?" she sobbed jerkily.

"What did he do to you, baby?"

Lisa let her hands fall and hang straight at her sides. "All he could do was hit me. I . . . I didn't care. It was that new one from Miami they call Pigeon who did things." The tears welled up and an expression of shame

58

clouded her face. Without looking at me she sank into a straightback chair and stared at the floor. "That one isn't normal. He . . . he's perverted. He made me . . ."

"You don't have to tell me about it."

"I never did anything like that before, even when they tried to . . . hold me down. He took this . . ."

"Can it, Lisa."

She looked up, her eyes gone dull. "They hurt me. Step laughed and laughed. He thinks I let you go . . . because of those times years ago." Like a slow motion picture she moved her hand and ran her fingers through her hair. A smile played at the corners of her mouth and she said, "I'm going to kill him some day. Some day. Yes, it will be very nice." There was a sing-song lilt in her voice and only then did I realize how really crocked she was. Constant practice with the bottle and an uncommonly strong constitution provided her with the ability to maintain a semblance of sobriety even when she was almost ready to go off the deep end. Her fear had covered it in the beginning, but now it showed through.

I said, "Where's Fly, Lisa," as gently as I could.

Little by little her eyes came back to mine. "Fly is nice. He always told me when . . . Step wanted me . . . and I would go away. When I was sick . . . he sent a doctor. Yes, yes. He stayed with me a week then."

"And how did you pay him off, Lisa?"

Her smile was unconcerned. "It . . . didn't matter."

"Fly's no better than the rest, kid. Where is he?"

"Are you . . . going to hurt him?"

"No." I leaned forward to center her attention. "He took something from me. I want it back."

She frowned, trying to think, then grimaced and said, "You . . . you hooked, Irish? You can get the . . . junk anytime."

"I'm not hooked, kid. I want that capsule Fly took. Where did he put it?"

"He needs it." There was a defiance in her face I knew I couldn't break.

So I said, "It's only sugar, Lisa. He won't get anything from it but trouble."

It wasn't Fly she cared for. It was the little guy, the creature, the beat-down thing that made him so much like she was herself. It was the two-of-a-kind feeling, people in the same foxhole, wounded and hurting with terrifying death at any moment.

"Is . . . it true?"

I nodded.

Without seeming to cry, the tears began an erratic course down her cheeks. "He put it . . . somewhere. For later, he said. Now he can't go to his place . . ."

"I know, Big Step has one of his boys outside waiting to cut him off."

Absently, she wiped the tears away. "He knows where Ernie South . . . keeps his supply. He was going . . . to break in and . . ." Abruptly, the tears stopped. "You know Ernie South?" she asked me. Some of the drunkenness seemed to have drained out of her.

"We met. He's a bum."

Her mouth tightened. "Irish . . ." she opened her mouth to say something, stopped, reconsidering, then said vacantly, "He's . . . his king . . . heroin . . . the worst of them all."

"Did Fly tell you where he was going?"

"Tarbush's Coffee Shop. Fly . . . he stole Ernie's key once. He had another made."

"He's nuts! Ernie'll chew him up. He can't pull a stunt like that!"

She grinned again and nearly slid off the chair. Her eyes were half closed when she said, "No?" then her head fell forward and I caught her before she hit the floor, Lisa Williams was out like a light but there was still that satisfied grin on her mouth. I picked her up, dropped her in the bed and went out, making sure the door locked shut behind me.

I had just reached the front door of the vestibule when I saw the outline of a figure on the other side. I flattened against the wall, deep in the shadows, glad the overhead bulb was out. The door swung open and the guy standing there smirked to himself. Briefly, I caught the wink of light from the open blade in his hand, then he closed the door silently and started back toward Lisa's room.

When I laid the barrel of the .45 across the back of his head he went down like a withering flower and I grabbed him before he hit the floor. Even in the semi-darkness I could see he was a pasty faced snake with all the evil inside him written across his features. The dark gray suit he wore was the kind they only sell south of Jacksonville and when I yanked the wallet out of his pocket I confirmed it. The driver's license was issued to one Walter Weir of Miami, Florida. I said, "Hello, Pigeon," and slipped the wallet back.

The car he had used was a beat up black Buick ten years old, still carrying Florida tags. Nobody saw me lug him out and if they did, nobody cared. Shouldered drunks weren't unusual around that neighborhood even in the pre-dawn hours. Pigeon Weir did me a favor in a way. It saved hunting up a cab. I drove six blocks North and three across town to where Tarbush ran his coffee shop, an unlikely little place popularized by the trucking crowd rather than the beats. Tarbush had been nailed twice for pushing Bennies on the teenage set and did a stretch in Elmira, but if he was letting Ernie South use his place for a storehouse it looked like he never cut loose from his old connections.

Pigeon wasn't about to come to for a long while yet

so I just let him slump there half on the floor out of sight. When I saw the silhouette of a roving prowl car heading toward me, I went down beside him and waited until it passed. Then I slid out of the car and edged toward the narrow alley that separated Tarbush's Coffee Shop from the garage next door.

A night light was on inside, a single low wattage bulb throwing enough of a glow to make out the array of tables and the short counter with its oversized coffee urns. But it wasn't the front section I was interested in. All the side windows were barred, and at the far end was the service entrance, a steel plated door that looked impossible to force. I swore under my breath and out of habit thumbed the latch to check it.

Without a sound, the door swung open inward. The .45 jumped into my hand and I was in with the door closed at my back and the darkness around me like a blanket. If anybody was there with his eyes already tuned to the dark, I could be a perfect target and if I moved, they could pick me out by sound as well. So I stood there waiting, the rod out and showing big and if they saw that, they knew one flash of gunfire would get a barrage back and it might not be worth the chance.

A full minute passed before I knew I was alone. I let my breath out slowly, listening to the stillness, then flicked on a match. I was alone, all right, but only in a way. Crumpled on the floor among the wreckage of cardboard cartons and scattered cans that had spilled out mounds of coffee was the pathetic body of Fly who lay there with his eyes wide open, his neck cocked at a screwy angle and a dark bluish welt on the side of his neck.

Somebody had cooled Fly the hard way. He had torn his clothes apart, ripped open seams and turned the pockets inside out and I knew damn well what he was looking for. But he never found it. Every last possibility had been exhausted and the marks of frustration were there marked by where the body had been kicked a half dozen times.

It wasn't Fly who had opened the cans. If he had, he would have found what he came for. Idly tossed aside were two plastic wrapped packets and it didn't take twenty questions to figure out what they held. Somebody had finished Fly's search for him, not knowing just what it was he was after.

I looked at the body again and saw the bruise under one eye and the smashed lips. The fingernails of one hand were streaked with blood and I knew why he died too. Manos Kekker had picked up Fly's trail somewhere but didn't know he was dealing with a hophead half-crazy from narcotic starvation and Fly put up a fight. It was his last. He was chopped down quickly and efficiently without knowing what it was all about.

The stuff that had been in his pockets was piled on the floor, in the middle of the odds and ends, a new brass key. The match burned out and I lit another, picked up the key and went to the door and fitted it in the lock from the outside. It was the type you had to lock by key when you left with an oversize barrel bolt on the inside. In his haste, Fly hadn't barred the door and left himself wide open for murder.

And the chase was still on.

I locked the door, went out to the car and drove it to the nearest subway station. I pulled in next to a hydrant deliberately, took the knife Pigeon was going to use on Lisa, wrapped a handkerchief around it, and rammed it up to the hilt in his tail. He never even moaned, but he would tomorrow, and he'd get the message loud and clear. I wiped the wheel clean, got out and went down the Kiosk to catch the downtown local.

63

Chapter 6

Statistics say half of all police cases are solved through the use of informants. There are three kinds: stoolies who squeal to ingratiate themselves with the cops, those who talk when the cops put the heat on them one way or another, and those who dump information into HQ anonymously to get the competition out of the way.

But there are others of the night people who know the same things, untouchable in their own way, living by the strange code that separates those of the badge from their own kind. And I was one of them. Once. Until they found out different I'd still be one.

I got to the hotel as the day shift was coming in and I had a chance to get a quick glance at the desk. The night man was just coming on with wrists fluttering all over the place and he looked like a whipped child every time he looked at Ames. The lobby was empty and I crossed to the elevator and as I did Ames spotted, me came around the desk and took me to one side. "You have anything in your room?"

"Nothing worth while. Why?"

"Paul . . . one of the bellboys . . . spotted the fag going in there and let me know about it. I gave him a clout in the mouth. Either he was curious or he was after your skin."

I felt my shoulders start to crawl. "Listen . . ."

"It's okay. He tried that before on somebody who was holing up here because the fuzz was looking for him. Thought he could pressure him into playing his little love games."

"I'll give him pressure."

"Never mind, I took care of it. Just check your stuff. I don't trust any of those AC-DC guys."

"Sure." I slapped his shoulder, threw a dirty look toward the desk and watched the guy turn away with a nervous little squeal. Nothing was missing from the room, but I had run enough shakedowns to know my stuff had been thoroughly searched. Later I'd take care of the guy my own way and he wouldn't go snooping anywhere again.

I called the desk, got Ames just before he left and gave him Pete-the-Dog's number. He was in a state of half sleep it took a couple of minutes to lose but he straightened up the second I told him what I wanted. I gave him the poop on Karen Sinclair's kidnapping from the hospital and told him to spread the news to our people fast. There were always eyes around that saw everything and no matter how good you were, New York had just too many people who never seemed to sleep whose eyes caught everything and could put the pieces together. Some of those people were ours. Pete said he'd get on it and I flopped back on the bed and closed my eyes.

It was raining when I woke. My watch said ten after five and outside in the premature dusk of fog and rain the offices were beginning to empty, spilling their occupants into taxis and subways. I cleaned up, shaved and got dressed, then headed for the Grand Canyon of New York.

On the corner I picked up a paper, scanning it to see if Fly's body had been found. I was willing to bet it hadn't shown up yet and if the absence of news was an indication, I was right. I scrounged up a box, packed the heroin into it, wrapped it in birthday paper and addressed it to Newbolder at the precinct house. It wouldn't take them long to analyze the grains of coffee still sticking to the packets and locate their source. A few heads would roll and it was doing it the easy way.

Pete-the-Dog ran a newsstand that was a clearing house for anything we wanted. He always knew who was under the heat and where the rabbits were holing up and if somebody had to jump fast to stay ahead of the fuzz, he saw the message got through. We always took care of our own. I caught him having a hamburger across the street from his corner spot and climbed up on a stool next to him. "What have you got, Pete?" I ordered coffee and when it came, sipped it slowly.

"You pull some big ones, Irish. Good thing you got friends. Remember Millie Slaker?"

"She still hustling?"

"Yeah. So she leaves a client where they dumped the ambulance. She seen this guy get out and walk back to the corner where another car was waiting. Millie, she's in a doorway by now because she don't like the setup, but she hears the guy tell the other one to stop at the Big Top for something to eat before they go back. Millie got outa there then and that was that, but I checked the Big Top Diner and Maxine Choo remembered them because they was both foreigners. Now Maxine's a Hunkie, but she still picks up enough Polish to get the drift of their talk and hears them mention Matt Kawolski's place down by the bridge. They was both arguing about something like if they should check in and pick up expenses right then or wait. She got kind of busy then and when she listened back in they had decided, paid up and left.

"I sent Benny down to talk to Matt but with all the seamen dropping in his place he couldn't tell who was new and who wasn't, besides half the guys there never spoke English anyway, and Matt, he's too damn busy to bend an ear to somebody else's chatter."

I said, "Get a description from Millie?"

"What am I, dumb?" he asked indignantly. "Sure. The guy she made was average all around and you couldn't pick him outa a crowd except he had only half an ear. Maxine didn't see that side of him, but the other guy she said was a mug type. Tough, broken nose, that kind of jazz. You know?"

"It's enough."

"So you goin' down there?"

"Tonight. Keep some of our people around."

"Sure, they're on the street. They won't let up until I call 'em off, don't take too long. They still have bucks to make and it ain't easy. This World's Fair crowd is a tight bunch with their loot pinned to their pockets."

I looked at my watch. "It has to be fast." I threw a buck on the counter to cover the bill.

Pete-the-Dog suddenly grabbed my arm. "Hey Irish, Big Step softening up?"

"What do you mean?"

"Carney said he took his spotter off Fly's joint. Maybe he ain't out for poor Fly no more. All the time he had that punchy Martino staked out to nail Fly if he went home and now Martino is gone."

I started to put the pieces together and they fit nicely. When Tarbush opened he would have seen Fly's body and gotten to Ernie South. With the cache of H gone they wouldn't have time to play any fancy tricks, so with Big Step's help they must have rigged it to get Fly back to his pad and let him be found there. Nice trick in the daytime, but it could be worked. Right now Ernie must be flipping with his supply of narcotics gone. I wished I had had time to shake down the place completely.

I said, "No, he's not getting soft. See you later."

"Sure thing."

The darkness had closed in completely by the time I reached Matt Kawolski's place. It was a dirty joint on the corner across the street from the river that stunk of city sewage from the vents in the area, stale beer and just plain age, but it was in a handy spot for everybody from the day crew at the nearby newspaper to the night crowd of seamen, bums and escapees from a city housing project a few blocks away. I hadn't been there in five years so I wasn't worried about being recognized, and Matt wouldn't even tip his own mother to an old face.

I managed to snag Matt alone in the back kitchen and I didn't have to paint any pictures for him. Before I could ask he said, "Blue station wagon and a late model sedan parked outside Mort Gilfern's print shop. He don't get much action never."

"He the one that turns out that Commie newssheet?"

"Yeah, hands it out free to the seamen. Plays up trouble, goes for ship tieups, backs hardnosed union demands. I won't let him in here since he was in the May Day parade. Says he's a liberal, but I know what he is."

"How'd you hear?"

"Billie Cole said it." He threw a quick look to the half closed door and wiped the sweat from his face. "That guy with the half a ear . . ."

"What about him?"

"Billie saw him gettin' out a car. He been there before, Billie said."

"Thanks, Matt."

"You gonna bring any trouble in here?"

"Nope."

"Can if you want. Enough boys here to take care of it. They ain't all alike. Some of you guys from uptown are scrounging around too."

"I'll yell if I need them."

"Since when did you ever need anybody?" he asked and went back to cleaning out his pots under a steaming fawcet.

The rain had turned from a drizzle to a hard, slashing downpour. The fog had dispersed, but the cloud bank overhead put a ceiling on the city like sealing up a tomb. Small rolling rivers cascaded along the curbs to swirl down into the sewers and aside from a hissing of occasional car tires on the wet streets, all sound had been obliterated. Even the short blasts from tugs in the river or freighters at the docks were muffled and the jets circling overhead to come in at LaGuardia or International had no more than the soft drone of a bee then were gone.

Nobody was on the street. If they were, they had slouched back into doorways or found a dry spot in one of the abandoned buildings if they couldn't afford a beer inside a gin mill somewhere. I came out of Matt's alone, trench coat open, hat half sideways on my head, weaving up the sidewalk like any early drunk, oblivious of the downpour. In case anyone was watching I even managed to make myself sick and chucked my cookies up against a wall. It was a nice act. It got me past the old store where Mort Gilfern had his print shop and time to case it quickly. The windows were painted over and I knew the door would be locked, but through a chip in the lettering that spelled out Mort's name I saw a speck of yellow that meant he had a light on inside.

There was no back way in. The opposite street was a clutter of construction equipment and piles of rubble where buildings had been demolished with the debris still in gigantic piles waiting to be hauled off. A well lighted watchman's shack was on the site and inside a pair of uniformed guards were looking out the side doors.

One was still open and I took it. I scaled a fence on the other end, forced down a rusted fire ladder and swung myself up to the landing. The stairs leading to the roof were all but rusted through and I stayed tight to the edge where the support was greatest. They were all three story buildings, most of them empty, with evidences of summertime love nests here and there, rotted army cots and soggy mattresses with empty wine bottles thrown carelessly aside. I went over the parapets, keeping to the shadows until I was on top of the building that housed Mort Gilfern on the bottom floor. Ahead of me in the night was the irregular outline of the rooftop entrance.

Mort hadn't taken any chances. It was a steel fire door and bolted from the inside. The plating over it was fairly new and bolted in place. Unlike the other buildings, this one had no skylight. The only way down was the fire escape, a steel vertical ladder hugging the exterior wall fifteen feet to the landing and anyplace along it I would be a perfect target. I hated to lose the trenchcoat, but it was too light in color. I shucked it off and left it on the rooftop. In my black suit I would be almost impossible to spot unless a light hit me squarely.

The rain went through my clothes before I was halfway down. I made the landing and stood there a minute. Beside me a dirty window was locked in place, pigeon droppings and a mound of coal dust and grit piled along the sill showing it hadn't been used in months. I started to feel my way down the staircase to the next floor when I saw the thin line of light that reflected on the sandstone basement and then the lightning flash cut through the cloud layer above and I froze. The thunder came immediately afterward, a dull booming that preceded a sharper crack. I was glad I had the chance to immobilize myself there. Down below I saw the faint red dot that brightened once, the tip of a cigarette that flared as the guy behind it sucked in hard.

Between the bursts of light I went back up to the top landing, waited for the flash, and when the thunder followed it, rapped a hole in the window pane and hoped the sound wasn't heard below. It only took a second to open the latch and get the window up, then I was inside. These old buildings were built from identical patterns to exact minimum specifications and I had no trouble feeling my way to the stairwell outside the door. I went down the steps, sweating out each creak, pausing between sounds until I was on the second floor.

The door on my left was shut, but the warp in it bowed it inwards and the light in the gap showed no sign of a chain across it. I knew they'd have it locked but that wouldn't be any trouble at all. It would have to be quick and it would have to be exact. There wouldn't be time for second chances. These were pros trained in a school that specialized in perfection and they wouldn't be just sitting there idly.

As softly as I could I edged up close, the .45 cocked in my fist. Inside there was a choked sob and a harsh voice said abruptly, "Be still!" There was a foreign rasp to his words I couldn't quite place.

There was another sob and I knew I had guessed right. It was a woman and it could be only one. This time it was the other voice that said in the same accent, "Lady, I will make you be quiet!"

He might have. I heard a chair scrape back when the other one rattled something off in what sounded like Polish and at the same time I blasted the lock off the door with the .45 and smashed the door wide open with my foot so that it splintered with a dry crack and dangled from one hinge.

They spun together and I had time to see that only one had a gun beside him on the tabletop. I blew his whole face into a bloody froth with the first shot and as the other one unlimbered a Luger from his belt already thinking he had me I took him through the chest dead center and he half flew backwards across the room as he screamed *"Alex!"* just once. He was dead before his head made a sodden sound against the radiator and I didn't stand there waiting. I triggered three shots fast into the floor, backed out into the hall, listened a minute and went down the stairs fast and waited.

Maybe it took ten seconds, maybe less, but I was there first. The one who had been outside came in with all the stupidity that initial excitement brings on and forgot the rules. He remembered them a moment too late and by then he felt the gun in the back of his neck and his knees went limp with fear because he knew there was no sportsmanship in this game and he would be dead before he could move.

I said, "Upstairs," and went behind him, the .45 barely nudging his spine right above his belt. He let out little whining noises and when he saw the two on the floor he gagged, spilling his supper down the front of his suit.

Karen Sinclair lay on a rumpled bed still wrapped in a white hospital gown. A dirty blanket was thrown carelessly over her legs and her hands were taped together on her stomach. Both ankles were taped too, the strip running around the metal framework of the bed.

Someone had wanted to see what she looked like and the gown was pulled up to her navel. She was conscious now, her eyes wide open . . . and now she was beautiful. I kept the gun on the guy, pulled the gown down, flicked open the blade I carried in my pocket and sliced through the tape around her wrists and ankles. She smiled, never taking her eyes from me.

Very slowly then I turned and looked at the face of the one who had been outside.

Their eyes always got that way when they knew they were about to die. It was a dull, glassy look and a slack expression and no words because they realized that the one on the other end of the gun had the same conscience factor as they had themselves and would shoot for the fun of it if they had to. They could hardly

72

talk with the fear, so they couldn't lie at all. They could only hope that it would be over fast and painlessly and not with a gigantic hole in their intestines that would leave them living in hours of agony before the merciful blackness came.

I said to him, "Manos Dekker . . . where is he?"

A long string of saliva drooled from his mouth. He turned his head and looked at the mess on the floor. Outside there was another flash of lightning, closer this time, and the sharp roll of thunder. "He . . ." The guy stopped there, thinking about the rules again. He swallowed, wiped his mouth and let his lips come shut.

I lifted the gun and let him look down the big hole.

He saw it. He saw the hammer back and he could smell the cordite and the blood in the room. He said, "He went back to get . . . the thing."

"Where?"

And I knew he was telling the truth when the fear came back and he opened his hands helplessly. The fear was too big to let him lie, the smell of blood too strong.

I reached out and turned him around. "Look at that one," I said."

Automatically, he looked down at the corpse on the floor, the one without any face left at all. Then I swung the .45 and laid it across the side of his head so hard the scalp split and blood and tissue splashed over my hand. He went down without a sound, falling so that he was almost kissing the faceless body of the one by the radiator.

I went back to Karen and said, "Did they hurt you?"

"No . . . not yet. They . . . were waiting."

"Can you walk?"

"I can try."

"Maybe I can carry you."

"It won't be necessary."

"We have to get out of here. It isn't over yet."

She looked down at herself, gradually swinging her legs over the edge of the bed until she was sitting up. A

73

grimace of pain went across her face, then disappeared.

"Wait a minute," I told her. I jacked a shell in the chamber of the Luger I took from the guy, threw it to her and raced up the stairs to the rooftop and unbolted the steel fire door. I found my trenchcoat where I threw it behind the parapet and took it back down again.

Women. They are all alike. Death they could face up to, public nakedness . . . never. She gave me a wry smile as I helped her into it, then followed me down the stairs. We went through the print shop and I unbolted the door so the others would have no trouble. I found the phone, dialed Shaffer's number and got him after I identified myself. He said, "Where are you, Irish?"

"Down under the Brooklyn Bridge, a place called Mort Gilfern's Print Shop."

"We know it."

"Then hit it. There are two dead guys and a cold one here waiting."

"Did you do it?"

"All by myself, buddy. I have news for you too."

"Oh?"

"I'm shaggin Karen Sinclair out of here too."

"Damn you, Irish, you . . ."

I chopped him off fast. "You asked for this, friend, so I'm doing it my way."

He was still swearing at me when I hung up.

Going the eight blocks before I found a taxi wasn't easy. I had to stop a dozen times and let her rest, my arm around her waist. Beneath my hands she was a warm, live thing, big and beautiful, the gutsy type I knew she would be and each time she stiffened and I knew she was hurting bad I felt the pain myself.

The taxi took us up to the Woolsey-Lever and I went through the lobby with her, both of us putting on an act. The rain had soaked her hair into a lovely wet backdrop against her face and her laugh was a tinkly thing I hadn't heard before. The fag behind the desk gave us an obnoxious glance and returned to answer the switchboard with a sniff of disdain, paying no attention as we got into the automatic elevator.

I got her upstairs, into the room and laid her down gently on the bed. I undressed her then, throwing the trenchcoat and hospital gown over the back of the chair. Both the bandages were showing a little seepage of blood through the gauze and when I pulled the sheet over her she grinned through the hurt and let her eyes close.

Naked, she was too beautiful. Even a deliberate attempt to disguise it couldn't last long at all. I couldn't look at her too long, didn't dare touch her, and hated anyone that ever saw her like I was seeing her now.

"Can you wait for me?"

She opened her eyes, made a smile again. "Forever if I have to," she said. "How do they call you?"

"Irish."

"No other name?"

"Ryan."

"What are you going to do now, Irish?"

"I'd hate to tell you. Sleep."

"Yes, Irish," I arranged the coverless pillow under her hair and let her fall back gently.

Someplace in the city another person was waiting to die. He didn't know it yet, but he would. I knew what 'The Thing' was . . . and I knew where 'back' would be.

And now I didn't need any more help.

With her eyes closed she said, "Irish . . ."

"What, honey?"

"The only . . . record . . . of where those missile pads are . . ."

"Yes?"

"In that capsule. It would take . . . six months to . . .

75

locate them again . . . and it will be too late by then. I . . . can't tell . . . our people."

"That's what I thought. Don't worry about it."

I caught the barest glimmer of light from her pupils as she looked at me. "I won't."

Chapter 7

I loved the night. It was part of me, rain and all. It was an environment suited to me personally like it had been tailored that way and I put it around me like a cloak. I waved down a cab that was letting out a couple across the street, hopped in and gave him a street corner two blocks below Fly's pad. As we passed the Paramount building I looked up and checked my watch. It was a little after one.

Somehow the rain took on a new intensity, battering against the cab. The wipers worked furiously as if they were trying to claw through the downpour. I passed a buck over the driver's shoulder and got out, waited until he left and walked the rest of the way in total solitude. It was coming down too hard for anyone to be on the streets at all, even to look for a taxi and that's the way I wanted it.

The place where Fly had lived was in the basement rooms of a brownstone tenement, ugly places that were born with New York and now stood like decayed teeth in the jaws of the city. Cars were parked, nose to bumper along the curb, some junk heaps, others new and expensive from the newer apartments a few blocks away, the owners grabbing any available parking space as close as they could get to home. They would be lucky if they had tires left tomorrow.

I made my pass of the place from the opposite side, then crossed over and came back. I could be a target from a rooftop or window but I had to take the chance. There wasn't enough time left to case it thoroughly. When I reached the building I didn't hesitate, I took the short flight of stairs in two jumps, held in the shadows a second, then pushed the battered grill door back. I listened, but the noise of the rain didn't let any other sound filter through. The other door was already open, held against the wall with a brick.

With the .45 pushed ahead of me I went inside, feeling my way along the wall until I came to Fly's door. As carefully as I could, I turned the knob, nudged the door gently so that it eased back until it touched the arm of a chair and stopped. The only light in the room came from the street lamps outside, an ineffectual pale amber reflection barely able to reach through rain and filthy glass panes.

But it was enough. Fly's body was there, all right, his neck still at that strange angle.

It was more than enough too because it let me see the other body stretched face down a few feet away almost hidden in the deeper shadows of a sofa.

I stood there, crouched to one side of the door jamb, letting my eyes become accustomed to the gloom, ears straining to catch any sound. Little by little I could see the ruin of the place, the sliced open furniture, the scattered junk all over the floor.

No, the job had been done. Two dead men and a ransacked apartment meant that they had come and gone. I stepped inside, walked to the other body on the floor and turned the head to one side.

It was Big Step's watcher, Martino. I put my foot under him and flipped him over. Whoever had placed the knife into him had done the neatest, most professional job I had ever seen. It had been expertly thrust and Martino had been dead without ever knowing it. A few glassy-eyed steps maybe, but that was all. It was the kind of thrust and tear wound only a trained expert like Manos Dekker could deliver.

When I looked around the place I saw the similarity

78

of pattern there. It was like the back of Tarbush's Coffee Shop, every available hiding place being torn apart in the search, nothing missed.

And nothing found, either. The shakedown had started at one side and gone to the other, winding up at the door beside the upturned table. I grinned to myself because I knew it wasn't too late yet. That capsule was still hidden somewhere. Manos Dekker might know where ordinary people would stash a hot item, but he wasn't dealing with ordinary people. He was up against a hophead guarding his most valued treasure, his security against slow death.

I stood in the middle of the room and peered through the semi-darkness, objects beginning to become apparent. Dekker had done most of the work for me already. It didn't take much more. There was hardly an item that hadn't been ripped or smashed, taken apart minutely in the futile search.

There wasn't much to it really. Too many addicts used the same gimmick, each thinking they had pulled an original trick. I picked up the cheap ceramic lamp whose hollow base had been smashed open, knocked the dented shade off and looked at the bulb. It was unbroken, but not screwed all the way down. I gave it a couple of turns and it came out in my hand. The capsule so many people had died for was there inside the socket. I dumped it out and held it in my hand.

Behind me Big Step said, "Don't move, Ryan. Not one move or you have a hole in you big enough to throw a cat through. Lay that rod on the table. Easy."

And now it was over. All the way. The muscles under my skin were bunched and jumping and I knew there wasn't any use trying for the long shot. All I could do was stay alive as long as I could. I let the capsule dribble between my fingers unseen and heard it roll on the floor. Very elaborately, careful to let him see how I was doing it, I laid the .45 on the table and turned around.

Big Step wasn't alone. Ernie South was right next to him with a gun in his hand too and the smile he wore said I was ripe for dying any second. Step bumped Ernie with his elbow. "Close those curtains on the window."

Ernie nodded, walked around me and yanked the cord on the venetian blinds, then pulled the drapes over them. The dust came out in a small cloud and I thought for a second I might be able to move in the almost total darkness. But Step thought of it too and flipped the light switch on before I had the chance.

"I knew you'd come back, Irish. I knew you'd sucker yourself right into my hands."

"So I'm a jerk."

"A big one. We were waiting upstairs." He grinned at me slowly, his hate filled eyes black with a wild passion. "Killing Fly was stupid, Irish. You think you could tie us into it by letting him stay at Tarbush's? Ernie and me, we got him back here and when you put a shiv in old Martino you even did us a favor. So the cops make it out like Fly stuck him and he had a chance to break the creep's neck before he died."

"Where's the knife, Step?" I asked casually.

"Come off it, punk. Who cares? We'll put another one in the hole." He moved away from the door and sat back on the arm of the old wooden chair by the wall. "So you catch Fly raiding Ernie's warehouse. You figure he got more tucked away here and come looking for it, only you gotta kill Martino first." He gave a slow glance around the room, then back to me. "Fly did a damn good job of hiding it, but if Ernie has to tear this place apart board by board, he'll find it. That's just too much loot to throw away. And me, I got what I want, Irish, I got you."

Ernie said, "He stashed those packets of H, Step.

Don't you bump him until he talks." He looked at me, teeth bared with anger. "Or do you want to make it easy on yourself."

I shrugged, watching them both for any opening at all. "I don't have your junk."

"Suit yourself, buddy," Ernie said. "I'm going to enjoy playing with you." He got up and walked around behind me. I just started to swing when the butt of his gun smashed into my skull with a crack I barely heard before all sight and sound disappeared into a maelstrom of ink and I felt myself falling from a great height.

How long it was, I couldn't tell. I came to with a rush of sudden pain that swept down from the top of my head and invaded my whole body. My hands and legs were behind me and when I made a spasmodic move there was a tug at my neck and a cord tightened there almost shutting off my breath.

Big Step still sat there, smiling pleasantly, enjoying the scene. "The Capone loop, Irish. Every move makes it tighter. Soon you'll get a cramp and you'll be able to feel yourself die inches at a time."

"Where is it, Irish?" Ernie South asked me.

I let out a strangled sound and shook my head. What a damn fool I was! Big Step was right when he called me a sucker. I try it alone and blow the whole bit including myself. A woman I wanted and a whole world might die because I was a damn idiot. All I had to do was make a phone call.

Big Step got up, pulled the chair around so he could watch me and sat down in it, his legs stretched out in front of him. "Take it slow, Irish. This is for Penny and Little Step. My brothers." A look of pain crossed his face. "They was kids, Irish. You got them both dead. However the hell you worked it, I don't know, but you got them dead and you're paying." He glanced over at

Ernie and said, "If he goes out loosen up that cord and start him over again. We got plenty of time."

Ernie nodded agreeably. "He'll start talking a couple times around."

"Sure he will, won't you, Irish? You'll tell Ernie what you did with his stuff then I'll kill you quick for killing Penny and Little Step."

The voice from the door said, "He didn't kill Penny, Step." I couldn't move an inch except for my eyes. Ernie and Big Step both make quick moves toward their belts, but stopped halfway there. Leaning up against the door jamb with a flat black automatic in her hand was Lisa Williams and she was gassed to the ears, a drunken smirk twisting her mouth in a crazy smile, her eyes glassy, her hair in wet strings down her head. The broken nose, the scars on her face stood out lividly, giving her a frightening appearance.

Both Ernie and Big Step looked at each other, not wanting to take a chance with a drunk with a gun, but it was Big Step who spoke first, just trying to make enough conversation to get her off guard. "What you say, Lisa?"

"Irish didn't kill your brother, Step, but I'm going to kill you. I promised myself that a long time ago, and now I'm going to do it." She eyed the two bodies on the floor, looked briefly at me and her lips pulled into a taut snarl. "You had to kill Fly and him and now you want to kill Irish too. You damn louse."

"Look you drunken bum . . ."

"You didn't have to kill Fly, Step."

He half rose from the chair. "Put that rod away, Lisa. This punk here bumped Fly. You think I . . ."

"Sit down, Step." She pointed the gun at his middle, but still keeping Ernie in view. "You don't have to tell me anything. I can see for myself. I know things like I know who killed Penny."

Big Step scowled, seemed to crouch in the chair. "Who, Lisa?"

"Ernie South here." She looked across the room at him and gave a silly laugh.

Big Step's frown deepened and he turned to stare at Ernie. "What the hell's she talking about?"

I could see Ernie, too. He was sweating. "She's drunk," he blurted.

"Sure I am," Lisa told him, "But I know. You think he was Penny's friend? Like hell he was. You handed over territority to Penny he wanted for himself and he hated Penny's guts. He got him out all right. All he had to do was wait and when Penny went for Irish with his big mouth and what he was going to do Ernie killed him."

The sweat was really there now and Big Step saw it too. He let his eyes slide from Ernie back to Lisa and asked, "How'd you find out?"

"Fly told me."

Ernie stood up in a rage, his hands trembling. "A goddamn hophead tells a drunk and you listen to her? What kind of . . ."

"I think it makes sense, Ernie," Big Step said. "I heard noises like that from the boys. Moe tried to tell me and so did Carl Hoover and I wouldn't listen, but I'm listening now." His hand moved closer to his belt when he turned back to Lisa. "How did Fly know, Lisa?"

She laughed again, never taking the gun off him. "He saw him. He was looking for him to hit him up for some H and saw him. He was saving the story until he wanted to put some real heat on Ernie for a big bundle, only now he'll never be able to do it." Her face changed slowly and tears ran down the side of her face. "You killed Fly like you did me and now you go, Step."

The flat look on Big Step's face I had seen before. It

was a death look and it was aimed at Ernie South. The narcotics dealer went white as the powder he peddled and every cord in his neck stood out like fingers. "Damn you, Lisa . . . she's lying . . . she's . . ." He never finished. His hand streaked for the gun in his belt, found and fired it in a split second and doubled Lisa up in the doorway as the slug took her right in the stomach.

But the sound of it was lost in the bigger roar of Step's rod that bucked in his hand and put a hole in Ernie South's temple and drove him over the arm of the couch. He got up then, smiling like it was an everyday occurrence, thumbed back the hammer and walked over to me. "Too bad, Irish, but I can't leave you here to talk, y'know?" He pointed the gun at my head and I closed my eyes.

The blast came, a sharp, flat crack and I felt the concussion on my cheeks. There was no pain, no sensation at all. I forced my eyes open, looked up, hardly able to breath. Above me Big Step Stipetto was arching in the final dance of death, his eyes staring in disbelief, the hole that went through his neck from back to front pumping blood furiously until the torn spinal cord got its last message through to his brain and he crumpled in a heap, dead.

In back of him Lisa still held the smoking automatic in her hand, every muscle in her body wracked with pain.

I couldn't tell her. I had to hope she could see what had to be done. And it was her still present hatred of Big Step that made her do it before she died. She had to undo anything he had done and somehow she inched across the floor until she reached me and I felt her fingers fumble the loop from my neck. With her last remaining energy she unknotted my wrists, smiled wistfully and fell back.

"Thanks, honey," I said, and touched her face gently.

I let the feeling come back in my hands and finished untying my ankles. When it was done I knelt down beside her. "Don't move, kid, I'll get a doctor."

She let her eyes come open and the drunkness was gone from them now. There was a new look in its stead. "No use, Irish. It's better this way."

"Lisa . . ."

"Kiss me goodbye, Irish?" Somehow there was no smashed nose, no scars, and she looked like she must have when she was a Broadway star. Gently, I leaned down, touched my lips to hers, then her face relaxed while I watched her and she took her last curtain call.

I found the capsule where I dropped it, wrenched it apart and made sure the microfilm was still there, then put it back together and stuck it in my pocket. Outside I heard the wail of sirens and cut for the door. I had to beat the cops out or I'd be held sure as hell and the big killer was still loose. I pulled the grill back, started up the steps when the wall powdered beside me and I heard the crack of a gun from across the street. I was pinned there with no chance of breaking out and the first squad car came to a screaming halt at the curb. I took the cap out of my pocket, dropped it in the cuff of my pants and waited.

Newbolder and Schmidt didn't want to believe me. Five corpses were in the room and I was there alive with a .45 in my belt and to them it was all cut and dried. They had me where the hair was short and were enjoying it. But it was the move with the packets of heroin that turned the trick. When I asked Newbolder who he thought mailed them in and why, he stopped Schmidt's impatient move to get me in a squad car and said, "Keep talking, Irish."

"Not me. There's no time. You just get a call through on your radio." I gave him Shaffer's number and said,

"Your office will know who it is. If you tie me up now there will be hell to pay tomorrow."

Schmidt grabbed my arm. "Let him do his talking downtown."

"No, wait a minute," Newbolder said. "This whole thing's screwy enough right now and I don't want to go on a chopping block when we can clear it now. You keep him here." He looked at Shaffer's card in his fingers thoughtfully and went outside through the crowd to his car.

He took about five minutes and when he came back his face was screwed up into a puzzled mask and he was shaking his head. "How the living hell do you do it, Ryan? How the hell do you work it?"

Schmidt said, "What's the pitch?"

"Later, I'll tell you later. Let him go."

"Are you nuts?"

"No, but you will be if you don't keep your hands off. Okay, Ryan, take off. Tomorrow we'll get a report. A personal one. I'll want that whole agency staff present with every document of authorization they have to make this one stand up. I want to hear this from front to end and get it in writing so I can read it every time I think there's an angle I don't know about. Now get your tail out of here to wherever you're going before I change my mind and take a chance of being caught in the wringer." He handed me the gun with a look of disgust and I walked out. Before I hit the street I got the capsule back and stuck it in my pocket.

I didn't wait for the elevator. I went up the stairs to my floor and half ran down the corridor. Then I stopped. The door stood open an inch and when I shoved it back I could see the whole interior of the room in the bright light from the overhead, bed and all.

Karen Sinclair was gone.

86

I walked in slowly, stood looking at the open window that led out to the fire escape, then switched off the light. The wind had changed direction and a sheet of rain came through and whipped across the floor. I peered out into the night, swearing at the blackness for the first time. They had time and they had the room. I had been delayed long enough for the snatch to be made and there was no way in the world of telling where they had taken her.

I slumped down on the bed, my face in my hands, trying to figure it out. Somehow I had left a trail in the hotel and they picked it up. But how? Damn it, I wasn't that sloppy. I had been the route too many times. One mistake somewhere along the line. That was all it took.

How long I sat there I couldn't tell. The floor and end of the bed was soaked, my shoes and pants legs drenched. Then the phone rang. Unconsciously, out of habit, I picked it up. "Hello." The voice didn't sound like my own at all.

"Good evening," the other one said. The voice was harsh with a curious accent, the tone inviting like it was waiting to be asked to tell a huge joke.

I sat up slowly, feeling the chill run down my back. "Manos Dekker," I said.

"You are a hard man to kill," he told me pleasantly. I waited, not trusting my voice. "You have something I want. I have something you want. I believe a trade is in order."

I went to answer him and a pair of clicks, a piece of a word interrupted the connection before it was re-established and I said, "I'll deliver. How?" I had no choice. No choice at all.

"Ah, that is very good. Then we shall arrange it."

"Let me speak to her first. I'm not paying for a dead body."

I knew she'd be alive. He'd know I'd insist upon it. He

called out, speaking away from the phone and once again the connection was interrupted for a split second, then I heard her voice saying, "Don't do it, Irish."

Manos Dekker laughed softly to himself. "Oh, he will do it all right. He is a very decent American. He is like all the others of his kind. Very sentimental."

"Okay, Dekker, you call it."

"Yes, I will," he laughed again. "I will call you back within minutes and tell you what it is you have to do. I wouldn't advise any interference in the matter. You understand, of course?"

"I understand," I said, my voice cold with the fear in it. He hung up before I did and I put the receiver back slowly.

There was a flaw somewhere. I could feel it. I had it in my hand if I could figure it out. I took it apart piece by piece, bit by bit, going over the picture from the minute I met Karen, remembering every detail of the action.

It took a while, but I got it.

Now I knew where she was and how I was going to work it.

I jacked a load into the breech of the .45, thumbed the hammer back and went out to the elevator and took it down to the lobby. The little fag at the desk had his back to me answering a call on the PBX board when I reached him. I went around the counter and put the gun against his spine and watched him stiffen. He turned around, his face a ghastly gray, his lips quivering as he saw my face.

"You Commie bastard," I said.

"Please . . ." he lifted his hands defensively.

"How'd they get you in . . . use sex appeal? Or was it your hate for everybody in the world in general."

"I . . . I'm not . . ."

"Shut up. I saw a photo of you in a special file the Feds have on all Commie sympathizers. It was taken a while ago and you weren't in half-drag and without the usual makeup you didn't quite look the same, but I put it together. You even helped. You cut in on my talk with Dekker because you were scared stiff and loused up your connections at the switchboard there. When Lennie Ames mentioned my name you reported in like a good stoolie. They told you I was hot and where I stood and you were the pipeline. You saw me bring the girl in and got to them right away and they set the deal up right here on the premises. Cute, kiddo, real cute."

I let him see my best grin, all the teeth. I let him look at the snout of the rod and said, "She's in the hotel, buddy-boy, buddy-boy. I'm guessing she's in your room. Am I right?"

The look he gave me told me I was. I reached in his pocket, found the key. Number 309.

"Let's go," I said.

I wasn't in a hurry now. I was going to do this one easy and my way. We got out of the elevator, walked down the hall nice and slowly, the queer's knees dancing with fright. He was as bad as the worst of them in his own way and he was paying for it. I was willing to bet this wasn't the first operation he had been on and when he was checked out all the way he'd wind up with a dossier an inch thich and loaded with names. Too many people in the striped pants departments of Washington agencies played games with these types and wound up being patsies for a blackmail racket worked by the Soviets.

When we reached the door I eased the key in, the gun in his back telling the guy not to make a sound. I turned it, felt the latch go back and took the chance the chain was strung in place. Then I turned the knob, shoved the door open and rammed the desk clerk into the room with the flat of my hand.

He was quick, all right. The gun seemed to jump into his hand and the first shot took the clerk through the chest. And I had the time I needed. Manos Dekker saw the play and knew he couldn't make it and in a desperate attempt to wash it out the most horrible way he knew he whipped the gun in his hand toward the bed but before he could pull the trigger my .45 roared and blew the thing out of his hand, fingers and all. He looked at the bloody mess on the end of his wrist, no longer the killer he was, a fanatic with a political drive that matched his own lusts and made him a big cog in a big machine. He looked back at me, knew what was coming and tried to open his mouth to scream or plead or do anything to stop it. He opened his mouth wide and I shot him right through that gaping hole in his face and he slammed head first into the wall splattering his blood and brains all over the place.

Karen Sinclair looked up at me from the bed and smiled, her eyes bright and shiny. He hadn't done anything to her. He would have, but he hadn't. My luck ran just a little too good. I took out the capsule from my pocket and held it out. She opened her hand and I let it fall into her palm.

The way she looked at me and I knew I was looking at her said that it was just the beginning for the both of us. There was a long road to be walked and we'd be doing it together. The hood was gone because my own would never let me back again when the story came out and I had to walk the other side of the street whether I liked it or not. Shaffer didn't realize what he had gotten himself into.

Karen looked at the capsule in her hand as I bent down to kiss her. Her mouth was a full, wetly warm blossom that tried to envelop me, her tongue tasting me, one finger tracing a line along my face. I stood up and reached for the phone to dial Shaffer's number.

She said, "How many people are in New York, Irish?"

"Many millions, doll."

Karen looked at the capsule, then smiled at me, the beauty of her like starlight on a clear night.

"I knew I gave it to the right one," she said.

THE END

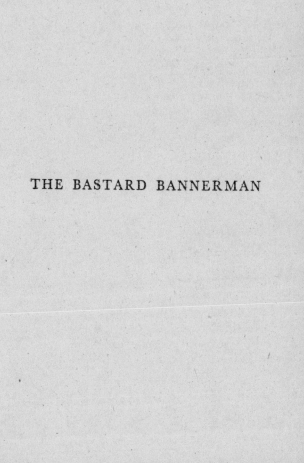

THE BASTARD BANNERMAN

Chapter 1

I let the old Ford drift over the hill so I could see the sweep of the Bannerman estate nestling in the cove of the bay with the light of the full moon throwing shadows from the tall pines and making the columns of the mansion stand clear like a skeletal hand.

The hedgerow inside the fieldstone wall that surrounded the place had outgrown it by six feet since I had seen it last and as I eased past the huge brick posts that had once supported a handmade wrought iron gate I could see what time and negligence had done to it. The gates were still there, but propped open, the posts ripped loose from the brick.

At no time did I have any intention of stopping by. Cutting off the main east-west highway onto 242 was an act of curiosity more than nostalgia, but when a guy lives the first twelve years of his life in a place before he gets the boot into the wild world outside, it's a natural thing to want to see if his old home had as many scars as he did.

Through the break in the tree line I could see the lights on downstairs. I grinned to myself, braked the Ford, backed up and turned in the drive and followed the curve of it up to the house.

What a damn fool I am, I thought. *Do I shake hands or slap somebody's tail for them? This was no prodigal son returning and if I expected a happy homecoming I was blowing smoke all the way.*

But what the hell, that was all twenty-three years ago, two wars ago, a lifetime ago and when curiosity gets the better of you, go to it. Like the old man used to say before he died though, just remember what it did to the cat. Then he'd laugh because that was my name. C. C., for Cat Cay Bannerman.

Now I knew the joke. Cat Cay was where I was conceived and born, only out of wedlock. The girl died an hour after I showed up and the old man brought me home with his name and a stigma the rest of the family couldn't live with.

The *bar sinister*. The bastard Bannerman. To be raised with the *bar dexter* class in wealth and tradition, but always on the tail end out of sight so the blight on the family escutcheon wouldn't be seen by the more genteel folk.

I parked behind the two other cars, walked up the broad flight of steps to the porch and pulled the bell cord. It had an electrical device now and chimed somewhere inside. When that happened the voices that seemed a little too loud suddenly stopped and when the door opened I looked at the tiny old lady that used to make me jelly sandwiches when I was locked in my room and tell me everything was going to be all right and I said, "Hello, Annie."

She stiffened automatically, looked up at me over her glasses, annoyed. "Yes?" Her voice was thin now, and quavered a little.

I bent down and kissed her cheek. It was quick and she didn't have time to pull away, but her mouth opened in a gasp of indignation. Before she could speak I said, "It's been a long time, Annie. Don't you remember the one you called your pussy cat?"

Her eyebrows went up slowly as memories returned. She reached out, touched my face, shaking her head in disbelief. "Cat. My little Cat Cay."

I lifted her right off her feet, held her up and squeezed her a little. The two day old beard was rough against her cheek and she squealed with a little sob of pleasure until

I put her down. "I don't believe it," she told me. "So many years. You're so . . . so big now. Come in, Cat, come in, come in."

"You haven't changed, Annie. You still smell of apple pie and furniture polish."

She closed the door, took my arm with fragile fingers, stepped back and looked at me closely. "Yes, it's you all right . . . the broken nose Rudy gave you, the scar where you fell out of the tree . . . your father's eyes."

But at the same time she was looking at the well-worn black suit and the battered porkpie hat and in her mind I was still the left over, the one who didn't fit or belong, who had always been a convenient whipping boy for Rudy and his brother Theodore, the family scapegoat who took the blame and punishment for everything two cousins did and had to cut out at twelve.

"Where's the clan?" I asked her."

Her eyes darted toward the pair of oak doors that led to the library. "Cat . . . do you think you should . . ."

"Why not, old girl? No hard feelings on my part. What happened is over and I'm not going to be around long enough to get any rumors started. Besides, there's not one thing I want from this bunch of Bannermans. By myself I do okay and no squawks. I'm only passing through."

She was going to say something else, stopped herself and pointed to the doors. "They're all . . . inside there." There was a peculiar edge to her voice, but she was still the family housekeeper and didn't intrude in the closed circle of affairs.

I patted her shoulder, pushed down the two great brass handles and swung the doors open. For one second I had that cold feeling like I used to get when I was told to report and knew what was going to happen. Uncle Miles would be pacing the floor in his whipcord breeches, slapping his leg with the riding crop while he listened to Rudy and Teddy lie about who let the bay mare eat herself to death from the feed bin, or who fired the old cabin out back. I'd know the crop was for me with long hours in the dark attic bedroom and a week of doing backbreaking man-chores to follow until I was allowed the company of the family again. I remembered the way old MacCauley hated to assign the jobs, but he had his orders from Miles and he'd try to take the load off my back, knowing he'd be fired if he was caught. If my old man had been alive he would have knocked his brother's ass off for doing it. But pop had died. He went under a frozen lake to get Rudy who had fallen through, caught pneumonia and a week later was dead.

But it wasn't the same now. Uncle Miles was a skinny, frightened old man who sat behind a desk with a tight face that was all bluster and fear and Rudy and Ted, a couple of pudgy boy-men with faces showing the signs of dissipation and easy living. Neither one of them had much hair left and their faces were pink and soft looking. Ted, who always was the lesser of the two, fidgeted with his hands at a corner of the desk while Rudy stood there pompously with his hands on his hips and his tongue licking his thick lips nervously.

There was a third one I didn't know who was relaxed in a chair with his legs crossed, smoking, an angular guy with thick, black hair and a pointed widow's peak above a face that was strong and handsome.

The other two I did know. One was Carl Matteau, the other Popeye Gage and they were Syndicate boys from Chicago and they both had amused, tolerant expressions on their faces.

Every head in the room swivelled my way when I walked in but there wasn't a sign of recognition on any of them. Miles and his two sons threw a quick look at the pair of hoods, wondering if I were part of them, but when Carl Matteau shrugged they knew I wasn't and Uncle Miles came halfway out of his chair with his face flushed in anger at the intrusion.

"Just what is the meaning of this!" he demanded.

I grinned at him, slow and deliberately. "A social call, Uncle. I came to pay my respects to the family. Relax."

It was Rudy who recognized me first. Something happened to his breath. It seemed to stick in his throat. "Cat," he said. "Cat Cay!"

"Hello, Punk." I walked over to him, stood there looking down at his eyes, knowing what he saw scared him stiff. He started to hold out his hand and I slapped him across the mouth.

Teddy never moved for a few moments, then skittered behind the desk. "Are . . . are you crazy?" he managed to get out.

"Sure, kid." I laughed and watched Miles let go the arms of the chair and sink down into the padded seat. He looked even smaller than before.

All he could say was, "*It can't be. It can't be you.*"

But it was and he knew it.

The one sitting behind me, the good looking one, came out of his chair very casually, strode over to the desk and stared at me with eyes as cold as my own. He was as big as I was, but only in height, but he had the kind of build you couldn't trust. A lot of those angular guys could be like whips. "Do you mind explaining who you are?"

I pushed him a little. "You first, buddy."

He rolled with the nudge. "Vance Colby. I happen to be engaged to Anita Bannerman."

Anita! Damn, I had almost forgotten about her. The distant cousin who was ten to my twelve, fair headed and frail who used to follow me around like a puppy.

She was another who had sneaked me sandwiches and milk when they had my back against the wall. Cute little kid. She had met me by the gate the night I ran away and kissed me goodbye and ran back to the house crying her eyes out.

"Well, how about that," I said.

"That doesn't explain you."

"I'm a Bannerman, buddy. The bastard Bannerman. You should have heard of me. Max, my old man, and Miles here were brothers. I used to live here."

"So." That was all he said. He nodded as if he knew the whole story and turned to look at Uncle Miles. The old man seemed to be in a stupor.

For some reason the whole thing got funny. Everything was out of focus and there was a charge in the air that you could feel on your skin. I said, "Well, I didn't expect any fatted calf killed for me, but I sure didn't think the clan would be so far on their heels they'd entertain a couple of bums like these two here." I turned around and looked at Matteau and Gage.

It was Gage who started to move until Matteau tapped his arm. "Easy, boy," he said to me.

I walked over to him, gave him one stiff shot in the chops and when he folded I laid one on the back of his neck that piled him into the rug. When Gage reached for the gun I jammed the barrel of the .45 in his mouth and felt teeth snap and saw the blood spill down his chin and the wide eyes of a guy who had just made one hell of a big mistake. He hit the wall, came off it knowing what was going to happen and too late to stop it. I let him have the gunsight across his jaw that laid the flesh open and he went down on top of Matteau with a soft whimper and stayed there.

All you could hear was the terrified silence. It was a noise in itself. I said, "Don't anybody ever call me *boy*," and I looked at the three other Bannermans who never knew any other name for me.

She didn't call me *boy* though. From the doorway where she had seen the whole thing start and end she half whispered, "Cat!"

My love, my little love, only now she wasn't small and frail. Darkly blonde still, but luscious and beautiful with those same deep purple eyes and a mouth that had given me my first kiss. Her breasts accentuated the womanliness of her, dipping into a pert waist and swelling into thighs and calves that were the ultimate in sensuous beauty.

"Hello, Anita," I said.

Even the pair on the floor, the blood or the gun in my fist couldn't stop the headlong rush she made into my arms and hold back the tears. I laughed, grabbed her close a moment and held her back so I could look at her. "I'll be damned," I said, "How you've changed."

Through eyes that were wet and streaking mascara she looked at me. "Cat . . . where did you come from? You were supposed to be dead. Oh, Cat, all these years and you never wrote . . . we never heard a thing. Why didn't . . ."

"I never left anything here, kid." I tilted her chin up with my hand. "Except you. I wanted to take you along but I couldn't have made it then."

"Anita!" Vance Colby was snubbing his cigarette out in an ash tray. He was the only one who seemed calm enough to speak up.

"At ease, friend. We're sort of kissin' cousins. Take it easy until we've said our hellos."

She seemed to see the others then. Like them there was a tension that came back over her, and eyes that were happy, clouded, and her fingers bit into my arm. "Please . . . can we go outside . . . and talk?"

I looked at Colby and felt a smile twist my mouth. I put the gun back and said, "Mind?"

"Not at all."

I pointed toward Gage and Matteau. "Better sober up your friends."

Chapter 2

The summer house had always been a place where we could find each other and we went there now. She sat in one of the big wicker chairs and I perched on the railing and said, "Okay, honey, spill it. What's going on here?"

"Cat . . . nothing. Really, I . . ."

"Since when do a pair of hoods sit in the Bannerman mansion? Grandpop or my old man would have thrown them through the nearest window and there was a time when Miles wouldn't let anybody in the front door who wasn't listed in the social register. So what gives, honey?"

"You . . . you knew those two, didn't you?"

"Sure I did. They're Syndicate men they call 'watchers'. They come in while an operation is being set up with Syndicate money to make sure it gets spent right."

"How did you know them?"

"Why?"

"You . . . had a gun."

"So I'm in the same business, that's why, but don't worry about it. What's the score here."

"I can't tell you," she said simply.

"Swell, so I'll find out myself."

Even in the darkness I could see her hands tighten into hard knots. "Please don't."

"I'm the curious type. Maybe I can stick something up Rudy's tail. He did it to me often enough."

"They're . . . not like they used to be."

"Neither am I, chicken. Now, do you explain?"

"No."

I slid off the rail and stood in front of her. "So tell me

and I'll blow," I said. "I don't want anything from those creeps."

Anita shook her head slowly, not wanting to look at me. "I'm afraid, Cat. They did . . . too much to you. Nobody can forget what they did. But please . . . don't make it worse."

"You make it sound interesting." I reached out, lifted her to her feet and put my arms around her. I tried to make it casual, a thing that cousins might do, but it didn't quite work that way. My fingers kneaded the firm structure of her back, my palms pressed her close and some crazy thing went through my head and down through my body and was happening to her too. She said something I couldn't hear because my face was buried in the fragrance of her hair, then my mouth was tasting her and feeling the wild response and fiery dart of her tongue and I had to shove her away with arms that wanted to shake.

"Cat . . . I waited. I never believed what they said . . . about you being dead. The night you left I told you I'd wait."

"We were just kids honey."

"You said you'd come back for me."

And I remembered. It was why I had turned off the road into the driveway.

"I'm too late, kid."

Her eyes were misty and she leaned her face against my chest. "I know. It can't be changed." She looked up at me. "Take me back, Cat . . . please?"

I left her at the door without bothering to go in. The black Caddie that had been in front of my Ford was gone now, the Buick still there. I got in the car, turned the engine over and drove out the way I had come. Culver City was six miles east and I had nine days before I had to do the job in New York and get back to the coast.

Outside of town I stopped at a second rate motel, put down five bucks and signed the register. I said I didn't need a receipt, got the key, the guy didn't even bother to look at the name and never commented on it, so I drove down to my room.

After a shower I lay on the bed staring up at the ceiling wondering just how badly I'd like to plaster Rudy and Ted all over their palatial mansion. I laughed at the thought because now it was ridiculous. I could take them both with one hand. I would have settled for a swift kick in the tail or a belt in the puss, dumped old Miles in the cistern out back and called it square.

Except that now a new note was added. The boys from Chicago were on the inside and the fun might be too much to miss out on.

I got up at seven a.m., grabbed breakfast downtown and at eight-thirty when I knew I'd get my party, made a call. Marty Sinclair came on the line with a gruff hello and I said, "Cat Bannerman."

"You in New York?"

"No, Culver City. I'm going to stick around a while."

"You and them crazy broads! When . . ."

"Come on, Marty. I used to live here."

"So why the call?"

"I don't know . . . something cute here we might tie in with. Look, work it easy, but see if you have a line into the local situation."

"Hell, man, Culver City is wide open. Gambling is legal, the horses are out of season but . . ."

"Can you do it?"

"Sure. Take ten minutes."

I gave him the number of the phone booth. "Call me back in fifteen."

He was right on the dot. Fifteen minutes later I knew of a Sid LaMont, had his address and was on the way.

Five sixty one River Street was a sleezy building on

the end of a line of apartments with a painted sign advertising a popular beer facing the water. On the ground floor was a printing jobber, a top floor with smashed windows, which put Sidney LaMont right in the middle.

The guy who answered the door was about thirty but looked fifty. He came up to my shoulders, peering at me with a ratty little face, hands fiddling with a dirty undershirt. These guys I knew how to handle without wasting time so I just pushed him back in the room and watched the sweat start forming on his forehead.

They always try a little bull at first. He said, "Look, mister . . . don't you come bustin' in here and . . ."

"Shut up." I didn't have to say any more. When I pulled out the handkerchief and wiped my nose he saw the .45 in the hip holster, swallowed hard and backed into a chair.

"Mac . . . I'm clean, see. I paid my freight. Ask Forbes, he'll tell you. What kind of stuff is this? I'm nickels and dimes. Last week I clear sixty bucks. I don't bother nobody. I . . ."

"Shut up."

I gave him the full treatment, going around the room, just looking until I was satisfied, then pulled up a straight backed chair, turned it around and sat down facing him. His face was wringing wet. So was his undershirt.

"Bannerman," I said. "What do you know about them?"

He seemed genuinely bewildered. "*Them?* Jeez, Mac, I . . ."

"Quick."

The side of his mouth twitched. "You . . . you cops?"

For a full five seconds I just stared at him until his eyes couldn't meet mine at all any more. "I'm not from Culver City," I told him.

Between my face and where the gun was he couldn't keep his eyes still. He said, "So they're big wheels. Live west of here. Hell, I . . . " I started to move my hands and he held up his for me to wait. "Okay, they're real fancy stiffs. You think I meet them? The two kids are always travelling with some hot tomatoes from the clubs and they blow the dough like it's water. The old one's a crap shooter and his brother likes the wheel. So what else do you want? They got the money, let 'em spend it."

I sat without speaking another minute and let him seat some more, then I got up and walked to the door. I turned around and said, "What do I look like?"

He got the message. "Man, I never seen you in my life."

"Remember that," I said.

*   *   *

There were five major clubs in town all located on the bay side. None of them were open for business, but somebody was in each one and when I told them I was checking on customer credit they weren't a bit backward about obliging me. I mentioned the Bannermans and all I got was a fat okay. They were big spenders and had been for a long time. They paid their bills and could get credit any time they wanted. They weren't big winners, though. Like any habitual players against the house they wound up in the red, but at least they enjoyed the pleasure of laying it out.

But I could still see the gates hanging off their hinges and picture the worn spots in the oriental rug in the library and it didn't make sense. There was just too much pride and tradition behind the Bannermans to let the old homestead run down.

I never knew what the financial set up was. My old

man's father had piled up the loot during the gold rush trade. He had made a find, exploited it as far as he could, then sold out to a company. He had split the pile down the middle between Miles and Max, but the old man wasn't one for investments when he could high tail it around the world chasing wine, women and song. Max had me and Miles nursed his dough. And that's how it goes. The snag in the picture was the gaming tables because you can always spend it faster than you can make it and the signs were that the Bannermans weren't what they had been.

I had gone through all the spots where you can usually pick up a word or two without coming out with a single thing at all. At a quarter to four I tried the public library on State Street, found all the recent issues of the Culver Sentinel and started scanning through them.

In two weeks there were five mentions of the Bannermans, all in connection with some civic project or social function, but not a squib about them in the traffic violation column. Three weeks back the headlines were having a ball because there were four rape cases, a hit and run that killed two prominent local citizens, a murder in the parking lot of the *Cherokee Club* and a raid by the Treasury Department men on a narcotics setup in town. The rapes and the narcotics angle were solved, three teen-age kids were being held for the hit and run and the parking lot murder was still up in the air. The dead man there was the lot attendant who had been fooling around with a friend's wife and the husband was being sought after. He was an ex con who had done time for second degree murder and had blown town the night of the killing.

Past that the Bannerman's came up again, but only in the society columns. There was one half page of notes and pictures devoted to the engagement of one Anita Bannerman to Vance Colby, a prominent realtor who had settled in Culver City some year and a half before.

When the library closed I went up the hill to Placer Street where the Culver Sentinel still turned out the only paper in town and walked in the bar in the next block, sat down and ordered a beer. A few minutes after five-thirty the place started filling up with thirsty types and it wasn't hard to pick out the newshawks in the crowd. But one was a guy I remembered well. He was a little weatherbeaten guy who had lost one ear when he and the old man had sailed the *Turia II* with a load of Canadian booze on board and the Coast Guard hard behind shooting with everything they had. The old man lost the boat and Hank Feathers had lost an ear and I had heard them laugh over the story many a time.

I waited until Feathers squeezed into what seemed to be a customary spot and ordered a drink, then I moved up behind him. I said, "If it isn't Vincent Van Gogh himself."

He put the drink down slowly, craned around and looked at me with the two meanest eyes I ever saw. Old as he was, there was a peculiar stance about him that said he was ready to travel no matter who it was. I grinned at him and the slitted eyes lost some of their meanness.

"That's what you get for sticking your head out a porthole," I said.

"Damn you, kid, only one man ever knew about that."

"And he liked to call you Van Gogh too didn't he?"

"Okay, son, who are you?"

"The bastard Bannerman. The old man used to tell you lies about my mother."

"Cat Cay! I'll be hanged." His face went into a broad, wrinkled smile and he held out his hand. "Yep, you got his eyes all right. And son, they weren't lies about your mother. I saw her. She was something." He grabbed my arm and pulled me to the bar. "Come on, drink up.

Damn if we haven't got something to talk about. What the hell you doing here? I heard you were dead."

"Passing through, that's all."

"See the family?"

"Briefly."

"All slobs. Idle rich and they stink. The girl's okay, but the boys and the old man the world can do without. They got too many people in their pockets."

"Come on, Hank, who could they control?"

He took a pull of the drink and set the glass down. "It's not control exactly, it's just that they've been here long enough to know where the bodies are buried and can play the angles. The old man wants a bit in the paper . . . he gets a bit in the paper. He wants opening night tickets to the Civic Theatre, he gets them. He wants his name out of the paper, he gets that."

"When does he want to be ignored?"

"Ha. Like when Theodore wrapped up two cars in a drunken driving spree and later when his old man had a statutory rape thing squashed for him and like when they interrogated everybody at the *Cherokee Club* after the attendant was killed. But not Rudy. He went home and no mention of him when everybody was listed in black and white. The power of social position, my boy, especially when wives try to climb the white ladder to the blue book and politicians need an in through an exclusive club in the state capital." He stopped and laughed. "But how about you? Where the hell have you been?"

I shrugged it off. "Ran away at twelve, tied in with a family of migrant bean pickers until they all died of the flu, latched on to a rancher in Texas who made sure I went to school, joined the Army . . . hell, I've been through the mill."

"You look it, son, you sure do." He cocked his head then, gave me a kind of sidewise look, his eyes studying my face intently and he said, "Damn if you don't look familiar. You do anything important?"

"I stayed alive."

"Well, you look familiar."

"I look like the old man, Hank."

He nodded slowly and finished his beer. "Yeah, I guess that's it, all right. Come on, have another beer."

"No thanks, I have to shove off. Look, I'll see you before I go."

"You better boy, or I'll come after you. Where you staying?"

I told him the name of the motel, threw some change on the bar, shook hands and walked out to the Ford. Things were looking up. The Bannerman's weren't as pure as driven snow after all.

Chapter 3

I had my own contact in Chicago and located Sam Reed who operated a horse parlor two blocks off The Loop. I told him to get me a run down on what Matteau and Gage were doing in Culver City and after the usual stalling he told me he would. That is, if he could. I wasn't worried about it. One word to the right people and his tail would be in a sling so he'd be in there pitching to get off the hook.

Then I ate supper and drove back out to the estate.

Annie was like a little bird that night, chirping and flitting around me. She had baked all the goodies I used to like and made me try some of everything before I could get out of the kitchen. Miles, Rudy and Teddy had stayed in town attending to business, but Anita was upstairs in her room.

I tapped on the door, went in when she called and smiled at the lovely doll brushing her hair in front of the mirror. She spun, grinned and opened her arms so I could squeeze her right and said, "I've been waiting to see you all day."

"I've been busy, honey." I held her off and looked at her. "If I knew you were going to turn out like this I never would have left."

It was the wrong thing to say. The smile left her face and those great purple eyes were tinged with that funny sadness again. "Please, Cat."

I nodded. "Okay, kitten, I understand." I let her go.

"Vance has been good to me. It . . . hasn't been easy."

"Sure. But I just don't have to like it."

"I think you'll like him, Cat. He's respectable, dependable . . . and he's done so much."

"Like what?"

She turned back to the mirror, refusing to meet my eyes. "I'd rather not talk about it."

"Fine, honey, one word and no more. Whether he's a nice joe or not in your book, he isn't in mine. Anybody who would tolerate those hoods in this house is scratching me the wrong way. So it's your business and I'm not going to interfere, but something is screwy around here and when I go I'll know about it. What I do about it is another thing."

The brush stopped its motion, then she jerked it through her hair and threw it down on the dressing table. Without looking at me she said, "It isn't like when you left, Cat. They're my family. They're all I have. Please don't do anything."

I switched the subject. "You have a date tonight?"

"No . . . Vance is going to stay in town on business. Some property he's involved with."

"Then suppose we just drop the subject, take in a club, listen to some music, see a show and dance. How about it?"

Her smile was like music. "All right, Cat. I'll be ready in fifteen minutes."

"I'll be downstairs."

But I didn't go downstairs. I went along the balcony to Miles' room and pushed the door open. I took five minutes to shakedown his place and wasted each one. He was a clothes hog, had expensive taste and had nothing tucked away that pointed to trouble.

Teddy's taste was a little more flamboyant. He had a gun rack on the wall with two shotguns, a rifle and six pistols. There must have been a dozen framed pictures of broads placed around, each professional studio shots of the show girl types, each signed with endearing bits of garbage to their wonderful Teddy who had probably kept them in mink coats.

It was Rudy who was the image of his old man. The conservative type who liked the big-business front. I went through his closet, and desk and the dresser drawers, again coming up with the big zero. His bookshelves were lined with the latest novels, predominately historical and a set of legal tomes, just the thing any clean cut American boy would have around. The only thing out of place was an eight-by-ten photo of a well stacked brunette in a stage bikini and it wasn't signed. The back was tacky with rubber cement and he had probably swiped it from a display somewhere. At least he showed an interest in broads. I put the picture back and went downstairs to wait for Anita.

She was right on time, her dress a simple black thing that seemed to overflow with her, setting the dark blonde of her hair off to perfection. Just watching her come down those stairs made my stomach go hard and for a few seconds I felt all empty inside and cursed myself for having let the years go by. She had waited. *Damn it, she had waited and when I came it was too late!*

"Ready?" she asked me.

"Uh-huh. Where to?"

"Well, you said a club . . ."

"Tonight the best. After that it's peanut butter sandwiches."

"The Cherokee is the best."

"Let's go then."

About five miles northeast the shoreline jutted out into a peninsula an eighth of a mile long. Right at the tip the lights from a low, modern building fanned out into the dock area and batteries of spotlights lit up the parking site. Flanking the roadway on either side all the way in were tennis courts, pitch-'n-putt links and two

114

swimming pools. At the very end a sedate neon sign read, *Cherokee Club*.

Anita said, "How did you know where to go? This has only been up three years."

I didn't tell her I'd been there before checking out the Bannerman credit. "Heard about it in town when I was finding out how much things have changed."

The house was full, and had it not been for Anita I never would even have made the parking lot. Every car there was one of the top three and just as the kid attendant was going to brush me off and catch himself a paste in the mouth, a big guy in a tux came over, saw her and waved the kid away. He threw us a grin and a salute, said, "Sorry, Miss Bannerman, the guy's new here."

"He take the place of the one who got shot?" I said.

"Yeah, and gettin' help ain't easy these days. Punk kids is all you get these days." He stopped and thought a moment. "The other one was knifed, not shot," he added as an afterthought. "Drive up to the door. I'll put your car in Miss Bannerman's usual place."

I slipped the Ford in gear and headed toward the building. "Pretty nice having your own slot. You come here often?"

"Only with Vance. He enjoys the atmosphere."

"He gamble too?"

Anita looked at me sharply, but my face showed nothing. "Very seldom. He's on the conservative side. He prefers investments."

"Good boy."

Inside we got the same preferential treatment from the doorman and headwaiter alike. Before we could be shown to a table a heavyset guy with close-cropped iron gray hair came up smiling, bowed to Anita and gave me a single look wondering where the hell I came from. She introduced him as the owner, Leslie Douglas and when he heard I was another Bannerman the same smile he had for her he gave to me. Old suit or not, if I were a Bannerman I had to be loaded, I guess.

The dining room lay like a horseshoe around a dance floor, butting a stage where an eight piece band played quiet music. There were two bars, one catering only to the men, with the casino area taking up the entire second floor. The layout was professional. Not the loose Vegas or Reno attitude that would take anybody's nickel, but more on the Monte Carlo style, catering to a single class. Big Money. I felt as much at home as a cat in a dog kennel.

For two hours we drank, talked and danced. For two hours we were those kids again laughing about the things that had happened because now they were pathetically funny. For two hours I lied to her about all those years in between then and now because I didn't want her to know. And for two hours we were in love like nothing before and we knew it.

But there was nothing we could do about it. She had the Bannerman pride of honesty and I had the sense to keep my mouth shut even though I felt like exploding.

At five minutes to midnight she excused herself to go to the powder room and I waved for another drink. Before it came I saw the big guy edging over to my table, smiling and talking to the others on the way until he reached me. His nose had been broken, he had one twisted ear and under his clothes you knew there were great chunks of muscle that could hurt you bad if he wanted to.

He nodded at an empty chair and said, "Mind?"

"No, sit down. Want a drink!"

"Thanks. I'm on duty."

"Bouncing?"

His shoulders moved in a massive shrug. "It ain't really necessary. I just speak to 'em generally."

"That's the only way."

The guy was getting to something. He waited until I had the drink and leaned back languidly. "You got a rod on you, ain't you?"

"Sure," I said, "but it ain't really necessary. I just speak to 'em generally."

The frown broke into a hoarse laugh and he shook his head. "Like my kid says, you're cool, man."

"Got to be in this business."

"Ain't why I came though. Les told me you was a Bannerman. That right?"

"Sad, but true."

"Couldn't be old Cat Cay Bannerman, could it?"

I looked at him, trying to get his point. I nodded.

"Maybe you don't remember me. I got my face busted up in the ring, but I was different when I was a kid. Petey Salvo's the name. We went to the Ringdale school together."

I let out a laugh and stuck out my hand. "I'll be damned," I said. "Woppo Salvo, the kid who got his head stuck in the fence posts."

"You remember that?" he grinned.

"Hell, yes, like I remember the times you and me had it out in the lots for something or other. It's been a long time."

"Too long." He let his eyes go over my face. "You do some fighting?"

"Some."

"You look it. Stupid racket. How long you gonna be around?"

"Few days, maybe."

"Suppose we get together some time? Plenty things changed around here. You want to meet anybody, let me know."

"Good idea."

Petey Salvo shuffled the chair back and got ready to

leave. "When I first saw you come in here I thought I recognized you from somewhere. Guys I get to know are the ones shouldn't be here so I was gonna heave you until Les give me the nod. Then I figgured you was like a bodyguard to Miss Bannerman."

"She need one?"

"Her? Hell, she's the only decent one. It's those kids who are bums. The night Chuck Maloney got knifed and everyone got questioned he paid off to get hustled out of here and didn't even get his name in the papers."

I picked up my glass. "Maybe he stuck him."

"Yeah, that'll be the day. Maloney was an ex-marine and had thirty-one fights in the ring and when that powderpuff can close in on him I'll eat his shoes. He's strictly yellow, you know that. I saw a dame beat the hell out of him one night." He stood up and held out his hand again. "I'm around all the time. Look me up."

"Sure will, Petey."

"Stay for the next show. Real speciality number. Chuck Maloney's wife is doing a strip. Les gave her the job to kinda help things along for her. She used to do a circuit in the east and swings pretty good."

"I'll catch it."

Anita came back then, saw Petey leaving and said, "Company?"

"We used to go to school together, Ringdale P. S. where the Bannermans joined the *hoi polloi* to have the democratic flavor infused into their veins."

The lights dimmed then and a spot hit the dance floor. From the band came a sharp chord that was sustained until the M.C. came out with a hand mike and got everyone's attention. His announcement was brief . . . the Cherokee Club was about to offer its feature attraction for the evening, a blazing redhead who had set fire to stages all over the country and was persuaded to visit the club for a two week showing. And introducing, Irish Maloney and her drumbeat rhythm!

The bongos and the base started their beat, were joined by a single clarinet and out of the wings came the redhead. She was good, no doubt about that. She had crazy muscular control of every part of her body and could start a ripple going in her thighs that worked its way up her belly to her breasts and undulate back down again. She stayed there working the perimeter of the floor with her body inches away from gaping eyes for a full half hour until the drums gave out and she ran off in a wild burst of applause from everyone in the room.

She was interesting, all right . . . but the most interesting part was that she was the same doll whose picture I had seen in Rudy's room, only then the red hair had photographed brunette.

Anita said, "She was beautiful, wasn't she?"

"I like you better. Ready to go?"

"Whenever you are."

I paid the tab, got her coat for her, said good night to Leslie Douglas on the way out and picked up the Ford myself. The kid in charge didn't seem anxious to tool anything less than a Caddie.

At the house I walked her to the door, turned her around and said, "Thanks for the night, honey."

She was crying. "Cat . . ."

"Look, I know. I know the reasons and the answers."

"Why does it have to be like this?"

"Because there's no other way. At least you're a real Bannerman. I'm still the bastard, remember."

"Please don't say that."

"Why fight the truth? There are two ends to the family . . . stay with the big one."

There was a funny light in her eyes when she said it. "I may at that."

Petey Salvo came out at three-thirty when the casino was empty. We drove a couple of miles to a drive in, ordered hamburgers and coffee and after a few minutes of old times I got to the point. "Petey . . . what's with this Maloney dish?"

"Ah, come on, Cat, lay off her. She gave Chuck enough trouble. You don't want none of it."

"Who says I do?"

"Well, more guys get a stiff one for that broad than any I ever saw. She was always runnin' and Chuck was always belting some punk who went after her. She drove him nuts."

"Look . . . what about that guy the cops are after?"

"Him . . . Sanders? So he tried making a play for her and Chuck nailed him. He did it a couple more times and Chuck did the same thing. But the broad kept the guy coming back. She liked to see the action, that's what I think. Chuck should never've taken her out of show biz. He was better off without her."

"Rudy Bannerman."

"What about him?"

"He ever try for any of that?"

Petey bit into a hamburger and scowled. "You crazy? Chuck would've mangled him."

"So did he?"

"Ah, everybody tried one time or another. She used to hang around the tables a lot and you know how it goes. That Rudy makes like he's a wheel to all the dames and feels good when they play up to him, but he knew what would happen. Anyway, he's a damn drunk."

"So?"

"So when he gets loaded he's no good. I heard a couple of the kids he had out laughing about the guy. He's . . . he's . . . what's the word?"

"Impotent?"

"Yeah. No balls. Nothin' much else either. The

dames laugh at him. Big guy and he falls apart in bed and bawls." He finished the other hamburger and washed it down with the coffee. "What you getting to anyway?"

"A little matter of blackmail, I think. I'm beginning to get ideas about how Maloney was killed."

"Well, if you find out, let me know first. Him and me were buddies."

Chapter 4

The first thing in the morning I called through to Chicago and got Sam Reed. In a hushed voice that always sounded scared when he was passing out a line he told me he had checked through on Popeye Gage and Carl Matteau and found out they were sent to Culver City ten days ago along with a bagman carrying a hundred grand that was going to set up an operation. The bagman came back, Gage and Matteau stayed to make sure Syndicate dough was spent like it was supposed to be. The only odd note was that although Popeye Gage was one of the 'watchers', Matteau had come up in the organization the last few years and didn't take assignments like this unless he had a going interest in things. The word was that whatever the operation was to be, Matteau would run it. He was overseeing his product personally. The other bit was that Popeye had become a junkie and was pretty damn dangerous.

I told Sam thanks, said I'd return the favor and gave him the name of my motel in case anything else came up. He told me he would and broke the connection. Ordinarily Sam was close mouthed and it hurt him to get squeezed.

After breakfast I found out where Hank Feathers lived, got him out of the sack cussing up a storm until he knew it was me, then got invited over for coffee.

Hank lived alone in a small house outside of town. The old man and he used to laugh about their escapades with the women, but Hank never seemed to stick to one long enough to make it permanent. The place was small

122

enough for him to take care of and served as a second office when necessary, and offered all the comforts a bachelor type could need.

When we got settled I said, "You did the story the night Maloney got killed at the Cherokee, didn't you?"

"Yeah, two columns. There wasn't anything to say."

"Run through it, will you?"

He watched me over the coffee cup. "Damn if you aren't your old man all over again. Get a nut in your head and you can't shake it loose."

"Well?"

Hank put the cup down and spread his hands. "Nothing. The guy was lying there dead with a knife hole in his chest. No scuffle, no nothing."

"Motive?"

"He had a five hundred buck watch some drunken clown gave him and a hundred eighty some odd bucks in his pocket. It wasn't robbery. He must have known the guy and didn't expect a shiv."

"Could have been something else."

"Oh?"

"Maybe he just wasn't afraid of him. He didn't expect the knife, but he wasn't scared."

"The cops had that angle too." He sipped his coffee again. "Not me though. I'd say it came as a complete surprise."

"Why?"

"He had a pack of club matches in one hand. There was a single unstruck match lying near the body. I'd say he was going to light a cigarette for somebody he knew when he got it in under the arms."

"The police reach the same conclusion?"

"Nope. Where he was were a lot of butts and some loose ones that fell out of his pocket. He always carried them loose. They say he was going to light his own and the guy caught him in that position."

I nodded, thought it through and finished my coffee. "I'd like a list of people who were there that night."

"Sure, check out two hundred reputable citizens and see what you can find. I tried it. What are you after anyway?"

"Something named Bannerman," I said. "Rudy Bannerman."

Hank Feathers grinned and leaned back into the chair. "Why didn't you ask it? He was plastered. He had just dropped fifteen G's in the casino and got loaded at the bar. When the cops came they found him in the men's room locked in a toilet sick as a pig. He had puked his ears off and sobered up pretty fast . . . enough to get himself out of there in a hurry, but he couldn't have raised a burp far less than a knife."

"The cops ever find the weapon?" I asked him.

"Not likely. The police surgeon said it was made by a stiletto with a six inch blade three quarters of an inch wide at the base. With all the water around here to throw in into there's little chance of finding it. Whoever killed him had plenty of time to dump the knife . . . Maloney was dead twenty minutes before anybody knew about it."

"Nicely set up."

"Wasn't it though? Now you got something on your mind, boy. Get with it. I'll feed you, but let's you feed me too."

"Feel up to stepping on toes?"

"Son, that's my life."

"Okay, see if Irish Maloney ever had anything to do with Rudy Bannerman."

"Brother!"

"He had a picture of her in his room. Care to try it!"

"You just bought it, son. I hope you don't get hurt."

"I've been hurt all I'll ever be, Hank."

The Bannerman name carried a lot of weight. There was only one family of them in Culver City and whoever bore it was set apart as a special person to be considered in a unique fashion. And like all families who occupied that niche, little was unknown about them no matter what it was. From the docks to the country clubs, they knew my old man and liked him, but the rest were another breed entirely.

They knew about the bastard Bannerman too, but as long as he was part of old Max he was right and it was the in I needed. It hadn't taken long for word to get around once I planted the seed. All they wanted to know was that I was a Bannerman and I had plans.

I hit three of the largest realtors, sat through cocktails twice and a lunch and came up with a talker when I found Simon Helm and got the idea across that I was back looking to establish a moderate smokeless industry somewhere in the area. After a few drinks he showed me the maps, pointed out suitable locations, let me digest his thoughts and settled down to the general discussions that proceed any deal.

Vance Colby's name had to come up. Helm asked me bluntly why I didn't go through my prospective cousin-in-law to make a buy and just as bluntly I said I didn't like him.

"Well," Helm said, "I'm afraid a lot of us share your opinion." He let out a short laugh. "Not that he's greedy or crooked . . . I'm afraid he's a little too shrewd for us country folks. For the little while he's been here he's made some big deals."

"It figures."

"Now he's got the property adjacent to the new city marina. You know what that means?"

"Prime land," I said.

"Even better. If anyone puts up a club there the expense of a water landing is saved, it's cheap filled property in the best spot around with the advantage of having access to all major highways."

"That's an expensive project."

"His commission will be enormous. It would be better still if he did it himself."

"That's a multi-million dollar project."

"It can be financed," he said.

"Is he that big?"

"No," Simon Helm said slyly, "but with Bannerman money behind him it could be done. Quite a coup."

"I'll take it the hard way."

He nodded energetically. "I don't blame you. Now, when would you like to look at the properties?"

"In a day or two. I have them spotted and I'll drive out myself. If I make a decision I'll contact you."

"A pleasure, Mr. Bannerman. I'm happy you came to me."

"So am I, Mr. Helm."

Right after supper I called Petey Salvo and asked him if he could stop by my motel before he went to the club. He said he'd be there by eight and didn't ask any questions. I drove back, had a hot shower, shaved and took out the .45 and went through the ritual of cleaning it, then laid it on the table while I pulled on my clothes.

It was just seven forty-five when the knock came on my door and I opened it hanging onto my pants, figuring Petey was early.

This time I figured wrong. The two of them came in easy with Popeye Gage levelling a snub nosed Banker's Special at my gut and his eyes lit up like a neon sign. Behind him was Carl Matteau and the smile he wore was one of total pleasure because this kind of business was his kind of business and he enjoyed every minute of it.

"Back," he said. "Real quiet, guy."

I wasn't about to argue with the gun. All I could do was toss the towel I had in my hand on the table to cover up the .45 laying there and hope they didn't catch the act. That much I got away with if it could do any good. The only other thing I could do was pull the scared act and button up my pants just to be doing anything and Popeye Gage grinned through his swollen mouth and let me have the side of the gun across the temple.

Before he moved I saw it coming and rolled enough to miss most of it, but it slammed me back against the bed and I hit the floor face down. Matteau said, "More, Popeye."

He worked me hard then, his feet catching my ribs and my arms, but only once did he land one on my head and then he nearly tore my scalp off. He was laughing and sucking air hard to get the boot into me and every time he did all I could think of was how hard I was going to step on his face when my time came. He stopped for a few seconds and I made the mistake of turning my head. When I did the butt end of the gun smashed down on the back of my skull like a sledge hammer and I felt my chin and mouth bite into the floor and the ebb and flow of unconsciousness that never quite came. All I had was that terrible pounding inside my brain and the complete inability to move any part of my body.

But Carl knew when I was all there again. He said, "Talk up, wise guy."

"Should I make him?" Popeye said.

"No, he'll do it himself."

I dragged myself away from the bed, tried to sit up and tasted the salty taste of blood in my mouth.

"Nobody pulls the kind of crap you did and gets away with it," Carl told me slowly. "Now let's hear it."

I shook my head. I couldn't get any words out.

"You don't belong here. Why, punk?"

"I . . . lived here."

"Sure. So why'd you come back?"

"Vacation. I was . . . going east."

"Let me . . ."

"Shut up, Popeye. This guy's a punk. Look at him. Take a look at his face, all beat up. He packs a rod, he's got nothing behind him so he's a punk. He comes back to put the bite on the family like any punk will do only now he gets no bite. He gets wise with me and he gets nothing except his face all smashed in or a bullet in his belly if he tries to play it smart. See his car? Six years old. You checked his duds . . . all junk. Someplace he's a small time punk, a cheap hood and these mugs we deal with the same old way, right, Bannerman?"

"Look . . ."

It was almost time for Petey to show. I hoped he'd know how to play it.

"Out," Matteau said. "Tonight you leave. You stay one more day and you get buried here."

I was going to tell him to drop dead when he nodded to Popeye Gage and the gun came down again. This time there was no intermediate darkness. It was all nice and black and peaceful and didn't hurt a bit until I woke up.

And that was when Petey Salvo was shaking me. He was twenty minutes late. I was half naked and he was slopping off the blood and holding a wet towel to the cut on my head making noises like the second in the corner of a losing fighter.

I said, "Hi, Petey."

"What the hell happened to you? The door was open so I came in thinkin' you was sacked out and you're all over blood. You have a party going?"

I sat up, got to my feet and squatted on the edge of the bed. "Yeah, I had a surprise party from a couple of goons."

"Then come on, man, we'll nail 'em. You know who they were?"

"I know."

"So where do we go?"

"No place, pal."

He took the towel away and looked at me, his face puzzled. "You just gonna take it like that?"

I shook my head and it hurt. "No."

"So let's go then."

I pushed his hand away. "Let it be, buddy. I've had the treatment before. It proves a point right now and when the time comes I'll lay those pigs out all the way."

"How come you got took?"

"I thought it was you."

"Shit." He seemed embarrased. "If I didn't get inna argument with the old lady I coulda been here."

"Forget it. In a way I'm glad it happened. The guys who took me should have knocked me off. That's what they would have done someplace else. Only now they hand me walking papers and expect me to move out." I looked up at the huge hulk of the guy and grinned. "They got the wrong Bannerman. I'm the bastard, remember?"

"Hell, I know you ain't chicken. I just don't like that stuff. Why you take it anyway?"

"Because it ties in with Maloney's murder, kid. I want the one who did it and why. So stop sweating. This Cat got nine lives."

"Sure. How many did you use up already?"

"About seven," I said.

It took another scalding hot shower and a bruising rubdown by Petey to get me back in shape, but when it was over all I had was a small headache and a bunch of bruises. Then we got in the two cars and he did what I asked him to do.

He took me over to see Irish Maloney to introduce me

as an old buddy who heard his friend was dead and came by to pay his respects to the widow.

It was a small house with a small garden and a two year old car in the garage halfway down Center Drive. It wasn't much, but all the signs were there of a guy who tried to make the best of what he had in every way and I knew what Chuck Maloney really felt about his wife.

On the stage she was sensational, but meeting her stretched out on a chaise under a sun lamp was another thing. Oh, she had the lumps in the right places, the hippy curves and the full breasts that modern culture demands, the sensuous look that comes from Max Factor tins, but there were other things that took her down all the way. Clever lighting could take years off her, but up close you could see the years closing in, the tiny wrinkles around the eyes and the beginning of the flesh getting slack and the striations on the upper parts of her thighs where the skin had stretched sometime when she ate her way out of the burlecue circuit.

Yet inside her mind she was still twenty years old and all men were at her feet and she was able to prove it nightly at the Cherokee and forget that sheer professionalism and the help of electricians could put her across.

Petey said, "This here's my friend, Cat." He looked at me and conveniently forgot my last name. "Cat Cay. He was Chuck's friend too. He just wanted to talk, so I'll leave you guys alone. I got to get to the club. You got another hour yet, Irish."

I got the full treatment when Petey left; the way she sat up, took off the sun glasses and doubled her legs under her to make sure I got the full benefit of everything she had to show. The shorts were tight and showed the voluptuous V of her belly and deliberately low enough to show where she had shaved to fit into her costume. She leaned over to make me a drink from the decanter on the table, curving herself so I would be impressed by the way the halter held her breasts high and firm, pushing out over the top so the nipples were almost exposed.

Too many times I had gone the route before and knew the action so I could afford to ignore the invitation and when I took the drink and sat down opposite her I let her see my eyes and read my face until she knew I was what I was, but couldn't quite understand it.

I said, "Sorry about Chuck. He was a good friend. We were in the Marines together."

She lifted her glass, toasted me with a silent kiss. "That's how it goes."

"No remorse?"

"He was a little man."

"I don't know."

"He got himself killed, didn't he? This guy Sanders..."

She didn't let me finish. "Sanders was a nothing too. He couldn't kill a fly. All he was scared of was being put back in the pen." Irish Maloney downed the drink in three fast gulps and set the glass down.

"He wasn't a Rudy Bannerman?"

"Who?"

"Rudy."

"Him?" she said, "A nothing. Strictly nothing. A boy in long pants. He's good for a goose when nobody's watching and nothing more." She smiled at me, loose and wanting. "What kind of man are you, Mr. Cay?"

"Big," I said.

"Not if you were Chuck's friend. He never had big friends."

"In the Marines he had."

"Then come here and show me."

She reached her hand down and a zipper made that funny sound and the shorts were suddenly hanging loose down one side. She smiled again, her mouth wet and waiting and she leaned back watching me.

I stood up. "Thanks for the offer, honey, but like I said, Chuck was my friend. There should be a period of mourning."

I thought she'd get mad. They usually do, but not her. She giggled, blinked her eyes and made a mouth at me. "Ohoo, you *got* to be a big man to say no."

"Not necessarily."

The giggle again. Then she hooked her thumbs in the hem of the shorts, stripped them off in one swift motion, held them high overhead and let them fall to the floor. She let herself fall back into the chaise-longue in a classic position, still smiling, knowing damn well what was happening to me. "*Now say no.*" Her voice was husky with the beat in it.

"No," I said.

I walked to the door, opened it and turned around. She hadn't changed position or stopped smiling. Before I could find the right words Irish Maloney said, "I'm coming to get you, big man."

"I'm not hard to find," I told her.

When I was in the Ford and on the way back to town I knew one thing. I had found a good motive for murder. The thing was, how did it tie in with Gage and Matteau being involved with the Bannermans? There was one way to find out.

Chapter 5

I walked around the house and went in the back way where Annie was cleaning up in the kitchen. When I tapped on the door her head jerked up, birdlike, and she put the tray of dirty glasses in the sink and minced to the porch, flicked the light on and peered out into the dark. "Yes . . . who is it?"

"Cat, honey. Open up."

She smiled happily, pulled the latch and I stepped inside. "My word, boy, what are you doing coming in the backway? You *are* a Bannerman."

"Hell, Annie, it's the only way I was ever allowed in the house anyway. You forget?"

"Well you don't have to do that now."

"This time I did," I said. "I want to talk to you before I see them."

Her mouth seemed to tighten up and she half turned away. "If you don't mind . . . I'm . . . only an employee. Please . . ."

"In the pig's neck. You were the only old lady I ever had. If it hadn't been for you and Anita they would have starved me out long before I left. The Bannermans don't have room for a bastard in their great halls of luxury." I put my arm around her and led the way to the breakfast niche and sat down opposite her.

"Look, honey. Nothing goes on around here that you don't know. You have eyes like an eagle and ears like a rabbit and there isn't a keyhole or pinprick in a wall you haven't peeked through. Any secrets this family have, you have too, even if you do keep them locked behind sealed lips. That's well appreciated if it's for the good, but right now something is wrong and there's big trouble going on . . ."

"You . . . can only make it worse."

"Do you know about it?"

She hesitated, then her eyes dropped in front of my gaze. "Yes," she said simply.

"So what's the pitch."

"I . . . don't think I should tell you."

"I can find out the hard way, Annie. The trouble might get worse then."

She fidgeted with the salt shaker on the table a moment, then looked up. "It's Rudy," she said. "He killed the attendant at the Cherokee Club."

"*What?*"

She nodded. "It's true. He was drunk and he gets mean when he's drunk and doesn't get his own way. He . . . went to get his car and the attendant thought he had too much to drink to drive and wouldn't get the car and Rudy . . . went back inside . . . and got the knife . . . and stabbed him."

I reached over and grabbed the fragile hand. "Who says so, Annie?"

"Those two men . . . they were there. They had just driven up."

The picture began to form then. "So they picked up the knife after Rudy ran for it and they got the thing with his fingerprints all over it," I stated.

"Yes."

"What does Rudy say about it?"

She shook her head sadly. "He doesn't remember a thing. He was drunk and sick. He can't remember anything."

"And now they want money, is that it?"

"Yes . . . I think so. I . . . really don't know."

"Everybody inside?"

"They're waiting for Vance. Yes, they're inside."

I got up, gave her hand a squeeze and told her not to worry. Then I went out the kitchen, through the hall into the library where the clan was gathered looking like they were waiting for a bomb to hit.

From the expression on their faces, when they saw me, they saw the bomb coming. Old Uncle Miles grabbed the arms of the chair and his face turned white. Rudy, who had been pacing the floor with his hands behind his back, suddenly became too flaccid to stand and tried to look nonchalant as he settled on the arm of the chair Teddy was cowering in.

Only Anita seemed genuinely glad to see me, her smile erasing the worry look as she left the couch to come across the room with her hand out. I knew what she was thinking, all right; she could steer me out of there before I churned things up. But even she wasn't going to stop what I was going to do.

I hooked my arm under hers and went to the desk where Miles was glowering at me and sat on the edge. Everybody had something to say, but nobody wanted to speak. I looked at chubby cousin Rudy and said, "Hear you're sweating a murder charge, cousin."

That was the bomb going off. You could hear the hiss of breath, the sucking sounds, the sudden jerking movements as the words hit them. All Anita did was tighten her hand on mine and look down at the floor.

"How . . . did you find out?"

Over my shoulder I said, "Easy, Uncle. I just asked around. I saw Gage and Matteau here and put two and two together. To me they add up. Dear cousin Rudy's got his ass in a sling he can't get out of and it's about time it happened. I'm happy for one thing though . . . I'm here to see it. And it doesn't only hit the fat slob, it breaks down to Teddy and you too Miles. You'll never hold your heads up around here again. From now on you'll be the joke of the community and when they strap old killer Rudy there in the chair the Bannerman family comes to a screaming halt."

Rudy looked like he'd get sick. Miles kept swallowing hard, his scrawny chest gulping air.

"And me, Cat?" Anita asked.

"You're going to be a Colby, honey. You won't be wearing the Bannerman name."

"Do you think he'll have me?"

"Does he know about this?"

"Yes, he does. He's helping all he can."

"How?"

She glanced at Miles, wondering whether to tell me or not, then made the decision for herself. "He's tried to make a settlement with those men. He's threatened them and everything else, but they can't be moved. They . . . want an awful lot of money."

"How much?"

Rudy broke in, his voice weak. "See here, Anita . . ."

"Shut up, Rudy," I said. He did, and fast. "Go on, Anita."

"A . . . million dollars."

I let out a soft, slow whistle. "Well, it looks like Rudy's making a real dent in the family budget. What are you going to do about it?"

They all tried to look at each other at once. I caught the exchange and grinned at them. Finally Miles croaked, "We'll see that . . . it is paid, not that it is any of your affair."

"And what happens?" I slid off the desk, turned around and leaned on it and faced Miles down. "Rudy gets off the hook and the Sanders guy eventually gets nailed by the cops. He's got a prison record and a possible motive for killing Maloney. He's got no alibi and he loused things up by taking off when he heard of the killing. There's no murder weapon for evidence and the jury thinks it has a solid case and gives him the black verdict and the guy gets the chair. How are the Banner-man's going to feel then when they know one of their own is responsible for the death of two people now and the real killer is inside their own house?"

Rudy did get sick then. He let out a soft moan, grabbed his stomach and ran from the room.

Miles said, "What are you . . . thinking of?"

I straightened up and glanced around the room. "I don't know. I sure got an ax over your heads now. You beat me to the ground when I wasn't old enough to fight back and now I might have some fun."

"*Oh, Cat . . .*" Anita's eyes were bright with tears. She looked at Miles first, then Teddy and at Rudy who came back with a face as white as snow. "Don't do that to them . . . they're such . . . such nothings anyway."

I nodded, "Don't feel sorry for them sugar, maybe I can instill some character in them. Maybe Rudy will get an urge of integrity and decide to come clean."

One look at Rudy made that a joke. Rudy wasn't going to confess to anything.

I had something else to tell them they would like to have heard, but the entrance of Vance Colby stopped that. He strode into the library as if it were his own, immediately sensed the situation and said directly to Anita in an accusing tone, "You told him."

She let go my arm. "He found out by himself."

"And may I ask what this matter has to do with you?"

"If you're looking for a smack in the chops you're going about it the right way, buddy."

His smile was hard and the curious glint in his eyes painted the picture nicely. The casual way he walked up didn't hide the sudden bunching of muscles under his coat. He said, "Am I?"

And before he could start the judo chop I belted him in the damn mouth so hard the skin of my knuckles split on his teeth and he rolled twice before the couch stopped him and he looked up at me with a face full of hate as big as your hat. He was one of those over-confident types who had put too many hours in a gym wearing a Jap toga and practicing un-American fighting and he forgot about a straight right to the kisser. Hell, I'd had it out with dozens of these types before. "The next time I may shoot you, Vance."

I pushed my coat back to get at a handkerchief for my hand and let him see the .45. He didn't answer. He kept both hands to his mouth and tried to sit up.

"Aren't you going to help him, Anita?"

"No," she said solemnly, "I knew what he was going to do. I've seen him do it before. I think Vance needed that lesson. He can get up by himself."

Very gently, I leaned down and kissed the top of her head. "Thanks, kitten." I took her arm and started out the library. At the front door I said, "Look, I'd sooner see them sweat than start trouble, but don't you get involved in this mess. That Maloney kill is still wide open and there's no statute of limitations on murder. There's something fishy going on here and I'm going to dig it out. I want you to do me a favor."

"What, Cat?"

"Let me know what they plan to do. Everything, okay?"

"Okay, darling." She frowned at what she said, then smiled softly. She reached up and touched my face. "I can trust you."

"You won't get hurt," I told her. I kissed her mouth and the tip of her nose, but it wasn't enough. She was back there in my arms again for one fierce moment and it was us, just us and no one else. I knew my fingers were hurting her arms and I pushed her away feeling my heart smashing against my ribs.

"We'll make it, baby."

"No . . . we never can. I wish . . . but we can't."

I left her like that and went out to the car. At any time now the stuff was going to hit the fan.

At the motel I told the clerk at the desk I'd be around a little while yet, paid the bill up to date and went to my room. I double locked the door, shoved the .45 under my pillow, showered and flaked out with the radio playing softly in my ear.

Popeye Gage and Carl Matteau. They came to town behind a bagman who carried a hundred grand and it could be it was to set up an operation for Matteau. Luck played into their hands when they saw Maloney killed and picked up the evidence. His original investment had now increased tenfold if he pulled it off.

I reached to switch the radio off when the late news came on from the local station and the first item the announcer read off was that Guy Sanders, prime suspect in the Chuck Maloney murder, had been picked up in Seattle, Washington and arrangements were being made for his extradition.

Chapter 6

The morning papers had it all laid out. There was a full statement from the D.A. who claimed there was no doubt concerning Sanders's guilt and felt certain a confession could be obtained after an interrogation. He rehashed the details of the crime and stated that Sanders would be brought to trial as soon as feasible.

On the inside pages an editorial went through it again, crying out the need for justice and lauding the D.A. for his attitude concerning the affair. It looked like Sanders had had it. As far as the city was concerned, the investigation was over. Only the prosecution remained.

After I got dressed and ate I drove around for two hours checking out the properties Simon Helm had suggested to me, jotting down quick notes so I could have an intelligent though phoney conversation with him. When I finished it was a little after ten a.m. and I got to his office just as he was coming in.

For the kind of deal he was hoping to set up with me he was willing to forego all other engagements and took me back into his office with orders to his secretary not to disturb us. She had coffee ready, set us up and left.

"Now, Mr. Bannerman, how did you like the sites I pointed out?"

"Only two have possibilities," I said. "The old Witworth estate and the Flagler Hill section. However, they both lack one essential . . . a water table sufficient to my needs."

"How would you know about that?" he asked with a degree of surprise.

"When you know how to ask questions you get some great answers. It's my business."

"Well, I heard this rumor, but never gave it a thought. My, we have to find something else quickly."

"I'll tell you what I have in mind."

"Oh?"

"You'll have to investigate the deal . . . but it'll all be a matter of public record anyway. Check out that property my future cousin-in-law has next to the proposed city marina."

"But Mr. Bannerman . . ."

"For my purposes it's ideal. The building will be modern, handsome, the industry smokeless, the access highways are at hand . . . a railroad siding can be extended from the Tompson works and the benefits to the city will be far greater than that of another gambling casino."

"But . . ."

"No buts, Mr. Helm. If you don't want to handle it there are others."

He couldn't fight that attitude. He shrugged and drank his coffee. "Very well, I'll see how far things have gone. However, if it is not possible . . ."

"Then I'll have to take something else," I finished for him. "How long will it take?"

He glanced at the clock on the wall. "If I get to it right away . . . perhaps this afternoon."

I got up and reached for my hat. "I'll be back later."

"Certainly, Mr. Bannerman," he said, rolling his tongue around the name.

Hank Feathers didn't reach his office until a little before noon. I whistled out the window of the car and he came plodding across the street all grin and crinkley eyes and got in beside me.

"Step on any toes?" I asked him.

"Well now, son, I don't know yet. I got up around the

Maloney place and funny enough I know quite a few people up there. One of our printers has a place two houses away and a garrulous wife. Anyway, after due poking around I come up with a lot of answers."

"Gossip or answers?"

"You do the separating," Hank said. "This Maloney woman has quite a neighborhood reputation. She made no bones about her conduct, rather enjoying the Madame Pompadour concept. She had plenty of visitors, plenty."

"Anybody special?"

"Don't jump the gun, son," he smiled, holding up his hands. "Rudy Bannerman was positively identified having tried to gain admittance on two occasions, both times while he was crocked. One, during an afternoon, he was seen for better than an hour in her back yard while she was sunbathing. The whole thing was observed and though he was well tempted by that lovely dish, he stoutheartedly left before the husband returned."

"Good for him."

"The suspect Guy Sanders made several surreptitious trips to visit Irish and twice was seen with her in a neighborhood bar. It's enough to hang him."

"They'll sure try it."

"But here's the interesting note. From a couple of very nosey sources, one an old lady given to staying up late and the other our printer's wife who has some odd habits including insomnia, I learn that there was one fairly common visitor to the Maloney household when the husband was on the late shift at the Cherokee Club."

"Any description?"

"Very little. He was always dressed in a suit or topcoat, wore a hat and moved fast. Generally he drove up, apparently at a specified time and she came out, joined him in the car and they drove away."

"Car?"

"What old dame can identify a new car at night? It was a dark one, that's all. They suspect that he was Sanders."

"Great. What do you think?"

Hank shrugged, looked at me and said, "The guy was thin . . . so is Sanders. Rudy Bannerman is chubby. At least it wasn't him. Anything else you want me to get in trouble over?"

"I'll think of something."

He opened the door and stepped out, then remembered something and said, "By the way, I bumped into a guy who wants to see you very badly. A friend of your old man's."

"Who?"

"George P. Wilkenson, the family solicitor."

"Wilkenson? Damn, he must be ninety years old."

"Ninety-three. He's still active. Anyway, I told him you were back and he said it was urgent you get up and see him. He lives back in the past these days and can still chew your ears off. He and your old man were great fishing buddies."

"I'll say hello before I leave," I said. "And hey . . . who's a cop you can trust? Somebody with a gold badge."

"Try Lieutenant Travers. Tell him I recommended him."

I waved so-long, drove back downtown and cut over to the Municipal Building that housed the First Precinct and went in and asked for Lieutenant Travers. The desk sergeant made the call, told me to go on back and gave me directions.

Travers was pretty young as Lieutenants go, but he had all the little earmarks that stamped him as a professional law enforcement officer. Tough when he had to be, smart always, cute when necessary and suspicious eternally. He have me one of those long slow up-and-down looks when I walked in, was ready enough with a handshake and an invitation to sit down and had I not left the .45 and the speed rig in the car he would have spotted it and shaken me down on the spot. He caught the name, but it didn't cut any ice with him at all.

"Related to the Bannerman family locally?" He held out a pack of butts and I shook my head.

"In a way. I'm a bastard." His eyes jumped up. "A real one . . . born out of wedlock and all that crap."

He sucked on his cigarette. "Yeah, I've heard that story. Now, what can I do for you?"

"I've recognized two Chicago hoodlums in this town, Lieutenant. One is Popeye Gage and the other Carl Matteau."

Travers watched me, swung slowly in his chair a few times and said, "I know they're here, but how did *you* recognize them, Mr. Bannerman?"

I had to grin. "Got in a little deal in Chicago once and they were pointed out as Syndicate men. They both have records and I thought you might like to know about it."

"Uh-huh." He took another big drag on the butt and laid it down. "We appreciate your being civic minded, but there's nothing we can do. Is there a complaint you'd like to lodge?"

"Nope, but since I'm considering relocating back here I don't want any Syndicate people moving in on any business I have in mind."

"Then don't worry about it, Mr. Bannerman. Unfortunately, in any state that has legalized gambling, there is a certain amount of outside interference and an influx of off-color characters. In this case, Matteau is clean and has applied for a gambling license although his location is not specified. Knowing local politics, I'd say he'll have it accepted. Nevertheless, he'll be well

144

investigated and will comply with all state and local laws."

I eased out of the chair and said, "Thanks, Lieutenant. It's nice to know we're all safe from the criminal element."

For some reason he gave me a funny look, his eyes slitted almost shut and grinned right across his face. "It's nice to be appreciated, Mr. Bastard Bannerman."

I laughed at him, threw a wave and went back to my car. Fifteen minutes later I parked in the rear of the Bannerman Building on Main Street and took the elevator up to Rudy's office where the receptionist told me she was sorry, but nobody could see Mr. Bannerman without an appointment.

When I said I was Cat Bannerman and she had no choice she reached for the intercom until I switched it off and she took one look at my face and thought it better to head for the ladies room.

My chubby cousin had a nice setup. All the accoutrements for the idle rich. A mahogany desk, antique furniture, a well organized bar, golf clubs stacked in the corner with parlor-putting devices in a rack on the wall, a couch under a row of book shelves, a stereo hi-fi set and TV built into the walls and that was the order of business.

Except for Rudy Bannerman. He was stretched out on the couch with a wet towel across his forehead and when he saw me he pulled the towel off and sat up with an expression of pure fear on his face.

"Hello, cousin," I said. I toed a chair in close to the couch and sat down. "You're shook, cousin. You're thinking of what it feels to be a killer. You're going through the pain of relief because they finally caught up with Guy Sanders."

"Cat . . ." He licked his lips nervously.

"I'll tell you, cousin, but first I want some answers.

Talk back or hand me any crap and I'll slap you silly. We're not kids any more. You're not a few years older and twenty pounds heavier where it counts. Now you're older and a pig and I can tear your ears off."

He couldn't take it. He flopped back on the couch reaching for the towel. I said, "You had a picture of Irish Maloney in your room. Where did you get it?"

"I . . . from the display at the Club."

"Why?"

He came up from the couch, his face livid. "I don't have to put up with this! I'm going to call the police. I'm . . ."

"Knock it off."

Rudy looked like he was going to have some kind of attack. He came apart in little pieces until his round body began to heave with jerky sobs and once again he went back into the contour of the couch and stayed there.

"I asked you a question. If you want the police, they can ask it."

"She . . . was nice."

"How often did you see her?"

"She didn't want to see me. I was a Bannerman and that tramp . . ."

"How often, Rudy?"

"A . . . few times, that's all. She . . . she didn't like me."

"I wonder why."

"She didn't have to say the things she did."

"How did you kill him, Rudy?"

His head rolled toward the wall. "I don't remember. I was . . . drunk. Sick."

"When did they put the bite on you?"

"Who?"

"Gage and Matteau. When did they make their offer?" I asked him.

"Two days later. They . . . went to father. He had

146

Vance see them. There was nothing we could do. Nothing at all." His voice trailed off to a whisper."

"When do they want the dough, Rudy?"

He was on his side now, not able to look at me at all. He was like a baby in bed, seeking the comfort of crib and covers. "Saturday," he got out.

Three days from now. To get a million bucks up meant a lot of converting and it wasn't going to be easy and here was this slob sitting on his tail crying. Whatever stocks and properties were going into the pot for this little venture must be damn negotiable to be taken so lightly. In this day of taxes and paperwork a million bucks to line a hood's pocket wasn't easy to lay hold of. Taxes alone on that kind of loot would be enormous.

"Who's handling the arrangements, Rudy?"

"Vance . . . he's doing everything."

"Why him?"

"Father is . . . sick. He gave Vance our power of attorney."

I climbed out of the chair and started toward the door. This time Rudy turned over when he heard me leaving. The pathos on his face was disgusting. "What're you . . . going to do, Cat?"

"I don't know," I said. "Maybe I'll turn you in and watch you burn."

*   *   *

Petey Salvo lived in the house he had been born in. There was a kid in a carriage, a couple more under school age tearing the flower beds up and a twelve year old boy sick in bed with a cold. The others were in their classrooms and Petey was trying to grab a bite and argue with his wife at the same time.

At least I got him off the hook in a hurry. A Bannerman coming to visit the Salvos was the biggest day in her life and when he introduced me the busty doll in the pink

147

housecoat with a headful of curlers almost broke a track record getting into the bedroom to get herself straightened out and when she came back she looked at her husband with a totally different look in her eyes and I knew from then on things were going to be different around there. Petey caught the bit too and winked at me over his coffee cup and told her to blow with a voice of authority and like a dutiful wife she left bowing and scraping like I was the baron of Bannerman Estates. Luckily, he didn't mention I was the bastard one.

He shoved some biscuits my way and I buttered up. "How're your contacts around town, Petey?"

"Like what?"

"Two hoods are in from Chi. I want them located." I gave him their names and descriptions and he took them down in his head.

"No trouble. Maybe need a day."

"Too long."

"So I put out the word and we grab 'em. These the same ones hit you in the motel?"

"That's right."

"I thought so. I was wondering when you was gonna move in. You never let yourself get took before."

"I had a reason, Petey."

"Figured that too. How do you want to work it?"

"Just get 'em spotted. I'll do the rest."

"Like hell, Cat. If this ties in with Chuck I want part of it."

"You'll get cut in, buddy. I have a feeling I'm going to need you."

"You'll buzz me in a coupla hours. I'll see what I can do, okay?"

"Got it."

Simon Helm had had visions of money dangled before his eyes. He was waiting for me with photostats of the records he had accumulated and all the additional information he had picked up. He pulled a chair out for me, got behind the desk and swung the folder around for me to view his massive efforts in my behalf. "There it is, Mr. Bannerman, but I'm afraid it's all too late. Vance Colby picked up the option on that property for ninety thousand dollars. The option to be exercised within three months. The property alone is worth in the vicinity of a quarter million and his proposed installation will go a half million, at least. At this point I don't know if he is acting for himself, or another party, but in view of his past and knowing his method of operation, I'd say he was simply first man in a deal. You understand?"

"I get the picture. The property is out, right?"

"Definitely. The money has changed hands. The option has been signed. I'm afraid you'll have to consider other properties."

I shoved my hat back and wiped my face. "Guess I'll have to. I'll take a run out and look at the other places tomorrow. Sorry to put you to all the trouble."

"No trouble at all, Mr. Bannerman. Take your time and if you need any help, just call on me."

"Thanks, Mr. Helm, I will. Count on it."

I got gas down the corner and put in a call to the house. Annie answered and when I asked for Anita, put her on. I said, "Cat, honey."

"Where are you?"

"In town. You have any news?"

When she spoke her voice was hushed. "Uncle Miles is in his room with Teddy. They've had people here all day and didn't want me around. That one man was here too."

"The older guy, Matteau?"

"That's the one." Very softly she said, "Cat . . . what's happening?"

149

"Trouble, baby. Where's Vance?"

"He just left. It was . . . terrible. They won't back down. They want all that money and . . ."

"Don't worry about it, Anita."

"I heard that . . . that . . . Matteau tell Vance . . . if he didn't get everybody straightened out somebody else would get killed. He's vicious. Cat . . . please help us, please. Vance is doing all he can, converting all his properties to help Uncle Miles. Cat, I'm frightened."

"Relax, doll. I'm beginning to get ideas. You just sit tight, hear?"

"I can't. Oh, please, Cat, do something."

"I will, baby," I said. "I will."

I hung up and stared at the phone a moment. A lot had fallen into place, now it was time to play the calculated hunches. I made a collect call to the coast and got Marty Sinclair and gave him the dope I wanted. I told him to push it and reach me anytime at night at the motel if he had to, otherwise I'd call him back tomorrow.

Then I went home. I parked the car, opened the door, walked in and flipped on the light. She was laying there naked as a jaybird on my bed with her clothes strewn all over the floor and a cigarette burning in her fingers.

I said, "How'd you get in here, Irish?"

"Told the desk clerk I was your wife." She held up her hand with the rings on it. "He simply looked at this and thought you'd appreciate the surprise. Do you?"

"Love it. You don't mourn long, do you?"

"Hardly a minute, Mr. Bannerman."

I looked at her sharply and she caught it.

"Cat Cay Bannerman," she said. "The desk clerk told me that too. Like you said, you *are* big. But you didn't know Chuck in the Marines, did you?"

"No."

"Then you must have come to see me."

"Right."

"Why?"

"I was checking out a motive for your husband's murder. A good nympho can get a lot of guys killed. I wanted to see how well you knew Ruddy Bannerman."

"And I told you."

I put it to her bluntly. "There was somebody else . . . not Sanders. You were seen with him several times."

"Mr. Bannerman, there have been many others."

"This one was there often. Late."

Irish Maloney wouldn't have made a dime playing poker. She frowned, thought a moment and said, "There was Arthur Sears. I liked him."

"What was he like?"

"Good looking, money, big fancy Buick, treated a woman real nice. He was in love with me." She grinned and squirmed on the bed. "He wanted me to leave Chuck and go away with him. He said he'd do anything for me and he meant it too. I like that, men wanting to do all those things for me."

"Why didn't you go?"

"And have Chuck slap me silly? Besides, he didn't have *that* kind of money. When I go, I want to go first class. That takes the big kind. He knew what I meant."

I walked over and sat down, stretching out my legs. Irish tensed herself and spread out all across the bed, her eyes languid, watching every move I made. "Why aren't you working tonight?" I asked her.

"Because I was waiting for you. Petey told me where you stayed. I told you I was coming to get you."

"Maybe I'll toss you out on your can."

"You won't."

"Why not?"

"You want me too, that's why." She reached her arms out. "Come, man."

I didn't want to, but it had been too long. I made all

the mental excuses, then I got up and went over to her. She was big and voluptuous and ready and I was there. And ready too. And I found out why any man could get a crazy desire for someone like her, even if he was Rudy Bannerman.

Chapter 7

I got up before she was awake, showered and left a note for her to get home and I'd see her later, then I went out and phoned Petey Salvo. It hadn't taken the big guy long to pinpoint Gage and Matteau. They were both staying at the Orange House on Main Street and had spent the night before making the rounds of the clubs winding up at the Cherokee doing nothing more than having a few drinks and watching the action at the tables. About two o'clock Gage had gotten pretty jumpy and Matteau had taken him out. Petey had the idea Gage was a hophead and had to go somewhere to mainline one and he didn't know how right he was. He was all for going down and nailing the pair in their hotel but I vetoed it and told him to hang on until I pulled the cork myself.

At the restaurant I picked up the latest piece of news. Guy Sanders was on his way back to Culver City and the trial date had been set. Time was running out on the sucker.

Hank Feathers was still in bed when I got there. Waking him up wasn't easy and he came out of the pad swearing up a storm. I even made the coffee and it wasn't until he had two of them down that he began to act normal. He was sore because he had to spend a couple of hours with Lieutenant Travers going over my history and couldn't find one thing to say except that he knew my old man, I was a Bannerman and that was it. I wasn't about to fill him in all the way and he knew it.

He said, "You sure raised hell downtown, son."

"It's about time somebody did."

"Fine, fine, but they dragged me in. When a Bannerman yells around here everybody jumps. You put the needle into Travers about those two guys and he's got the lines burning all over the state. You know the pitch?"

"Suppose you tell me."

"For six years the Syndicate has been trying to move in here. They got a few places started but the state pushed them out. So now they got a toehold again. Matteau's filed as a resident and even though they know he's tied up with the bunch in Chicago they can't prove it or do a damn thing about it. He's got power behind him and it moves all the way to the Capitol. Brother, this town's got trouble."

"So stick around and get a good story. You still ready to step on toes?"

"Bannermans'?"

"Anybody's."

"I'm a reporter, son. Somebody steps out of line, it's news and I get it printed. What have you got going?"

"Throw a monkey wrench into the Sanders thing. Make it look like a trial of political expediency. Hit the D.A. and get the paper to press for a full investigation . . . anything to delay the trial. Give it enough coverage so they won't be able to get a jury that hasn't read or heard about it. Can you do that?"

"Sure, but I may get canned and I'm almost at retirement age."

"Take a chance."

"Boy, do I live dangerously."

"Don't we all," I said.

Petey Salvo got me into the *Cherokee Club* before anyone was there and I headed for the kitchen. He dug around in the cutlery drawers a few minutes pulling out every form of knife they had there until he had a sample spread out on the butcher's block of every one. Most were of the common variety, there was one I picked up and scrutinized carefully before I put it in my inside pocket wrapped in a napkin.

"What're you gonna do with that?" Petey asked me.

"Give it to the police surgeon who examined Chuck's wound."

"The guy said he got it with a stiletto."

"Look at the steak knives, friend. They're speciality numbers and might do it. Instead of tossing the murder weapon away, suppose a killer simply put it back in service. A check shows nothing gone, a weapon was available, and what happens?"

"You got me," he said. "What?"

"A killer gets away with murder."

Because I was a Bannerman, Dr. Anthony Wember was willing to make the comparison. He was sceptical, but had to admit there was a possibility that the knife I offered might have inflicted the wound. He couldn't be certain because of the peculiar nature of the cutting and puncturing combination in Maloney's chest, but it was a thought and he would consider it. He had gone to great lengths to establish the nature of the weapon and a stiletto type it was; pointed, sharp along one length at least, straight blade with a rising center. He seemed to think both edges had been ground, but again, it was speculation. The doctor said he'd check it again to be sure and would make the information available.

At least to a Bannerman.

When we left it was time to do the other thing. Petey was all smiles when we got to the Orange House because he knew the ropes and how to work it and got a pimply faced kid in a bellboy's uniform to get the key we wanted. I knocked while he stayed out of the way and when Popeye Gage opened the door he wasn't a bit worried because he had a gun in his fist and said, "Hey

Carl, look who we got. The punk's back and asking for it."

Matteau looked up from his paper, put it down and stood up with a grin wreathing his face. "Couldn't take a lesson, could you, boy?"

"I told you not to call me that." I started toward him fast.

"Hold it," Gage said. He walked up behind me and let me feel the muzzle of the rod. I maneuvered them just right so I had them with their backs to the door and they didn't hear Petey come in and never knew he was in the room until he slammed their heads together with an unearthly crack that put them unconscious on the floor for an hour.

But it took us that long to shake the place down. We came up with three .38's, a half a case of booze and forty-two hundred bucks in cash, but that was all.

Popeye Gage was the first one to open his eyes. He saw Petey leaning over him and tried to fake it, but the act didn't hold. Petey dragged him to his feet and held him up against his chest and you never saw fear in a guy's eyes before unless you saw his.

I said, "Put him in the chair, Petey. We have something special for him."

"Let me give him something special, Cat."

"Save it for the other one. I know what will make this one talk."

Petey threw Popeye halfway across the room into an overstuffed chair and the punk cringed there shivering because he found something that didn't play out the way he thought it would and he was almost ready to hurt.

Carl Matteau wasn't quite so easy. He had gone the route before too and decided to take it cursing and swearing all the way, but no matter what Petey did to him he wasn't about to spill his guts. I was figuring on

156

that and let him go through the rough stuff until the blood ran down his chin and his eyes were rolling in their sockets and said, "We want the knife, Carl. What do we do to get it?"

"Go screw yourself."

I hit him myself this time. I laid one on him that sent him out of the seat to the wall and he sat there on the floor glowering at me.

"You hit the wrong one, buddy. You're in a trap now."

He said two words.

Petey gave him one then and he went out cold.

Over in the corner Popeye Gage started to whimper. Petey said, "They done it, right?"

"They didn't done it," I told him. "They were just part of it."

"I'll kill 'em if you want, Cat. We can dump . . ."

"No killing, Petey. Don't involve yourself."

"Chuck was my friend."

"So we'll stick them. Only don't let's take a fall, oke?"

"You're calling it, Cat."

I went over to Gage and stood there looking at him for a minute. I said to Petey, "You know a place where we can put this one? Some place where he can't be heard and nobody can hear him scream?"

"There's the smokehouse behind your place, remember?"

Remember? Damn right I remembered. I had taken enough beatings from Miles there often enough when Rudy and Teddy had made me take lumps.

"That should do it."

Popeye knew what I was getting at. He could see a couple of days going by without pumping a few shots of the big H into his veins and knew what would happen. His mouth worked until the words came out. "Look, I don't know nothing. I don't . . ."

"It's only what the other's don't know, little man. That's what counts. They'll all think Carl clued you in, so sweat. Sweat hard," I said.

We left Carl Matteau like that and drove six miles back to the Bannerman place and locked Popeye in the smokehouse. He went quietly because Petey laid a short one on his jaw and left him on a pile of sawdust. When he woke up he'd be screaming for a shot and would be ready to say anything if we'd get him a fix.

I had Petey wait in the car and took the back door route to the house again. Annie had a ready smile, her hands and clothes white with flour. She told me Rudy had come home sick yesterday and was still in bed. Cousin Teddy left town on some mission and Uncle Miles was in the library with Vance Colby.

Rather than push on in, I stood there, listening to the heated voice coming from inside. The oak doors were too thick to transmit the words but it was Vance Colby that was doing the demanding and Uncle Miles aquiescing little by little. When their discussion came to an end I pulled back, let Vance Colby through without him seeing me, and after he was out and in his car I went inside to where Miles was hunched up behind his desk, his face looking like he had just been whipped.

"Hello, Uncle."

"I don't think you and I have anything to discuss."

"No?"

It wasn't *what* I said. It was the way I said it. His mouth started to hang open and I saw his hands shake. "What . . . do you mean?"

We *did* have something to discuss, all right, but I didn't know what it was. As long as he thought I did he was on the hook, not me. "I got the picture pretty well laid out," I told him, a grin on my face.

Miles looked like he was going to die right there. He'd make a lousy poker player too. He'd said enough with his face to show me not to push any further so I let out a chuckle and walked out of the room.

Anita was just coming down the stairs, saw me and hurried, both hands reaching for mine. Her voice was soft as she said, *"Cat, Cat caught the rat."* When we were kids and she said that I used to chase her until I caught her and held her down squealing and kicking making like I was going to feed her a worm. It had been a great game.

"Hi, beautiful. Busy today?"

"Well, Vance . . ."

"He just left."

A frown creased her forehead. "That's funny. He didn't call me."

"Big business."

I walked toward the kitchen with her, my arm circling her waist. She fitted up against me unconsciously, her thigh rubbing mine. "He's been like that for a month now. He's . . . changed."

"Feel like doing a little touring with me?"

"Where, Cat?"

"Just around. I have some stops to make."

"Okay," she smiled happily, "let me get my jacket."

On the way to town I checked in the office of the motel to see if I had any calls. There were two, one from Sam Reed in Chicago and the other from Hank Feathers. I put the one through to Chicago first and got Sam at his place just as he was about to leave.

"Cat," he said, "I got a little more on Matteau. Guy I know pretty well used to work with him and when I got around to asking about him he let loose some odds and ends."

"Let's have them."

"The Syndicate didn't just move in down there. They were approached by somebody with a deal. They never would have touched the area after all the trouble they had the last time, but this deal looked solid and they went for it. Seems legit and Matteau is going to head it up. If it swings the Syndicate will get in good, but it's got to be legit. They can handle things once they're established. Now, that do you any good?"

"It makes sense, Sam. Thanks for calling."

"No trouble. Like I said, I'll be wanting a favor some day."

"You'll get it."

I held down the cutoff bar, let it up and gave the operator the out of town number for Hank Feathers. He was in a hotel a hundred miles away on an assignment they threw at him the last minute and had tried to locate me earlier and couldn't. I said, "What's up, doc?"

"Something you'll have to run down personally. The printer at the paper . . . the one who lives near Irish Maloney . . . well, his wife forgot to tell me something. One of her constant visitors backed into a parked car one night and never left a calling card. Minor damage, but she just happened to be coming home, saw the accident and took his license number and stuck it under the windshield wiper of the car he bumped."

"A neighborhood car?"

"Can't say. She didn't keep a record. She was just indignant about him running off."

"When did it happen?"

"A couple of weeks ago."

"Good deal. I'll see what I can do."

"One more thing . . . will you get over and see old man Wilkenson? He's bugging me on the hour. Get him off my back. So he'll yak for a couple hours about the old days, but then it's over."

"Yeah, sure. See you when you get back."

"Two, three days. No more."

Anita looked at me curiously when I got back in the car. "Are we going someplace?"

I nodded. "Making house calls. You're going to see an insurance investigator at work. At least I hope everybody thinks so."

"Why?"

"Because all this trouble the Bannerman's are in has an answer and it's not the one you think it is."

"I thought you didn't care about them."

"I don't baby, not one damn bit. Only you. If it touches you then I'm involved too. As long as you're wearing the Bannerman name it's going to stay clean one way or another. I told you . . . there's not one thing I want from them. I was out a long time ago. I'm the bastard Bannerman, I never had anything and never wanted anything. In a way I'm lucky. What I never had I don't miss. I can work things out for myself and although I don't eat high off the hog I manage to keep my stomach full. I'm free and clear because I don't own enough to get into debt over. Don't think there weren't times when I envied Rudy and Teddy all they had. I used to hate their guts because they had it all and took what little I had away too. But it's over now and that's it. For you I'm pushing, no other reason."

"I love you, Cat. I shouldn't say it, but I do. I always have."

"I know, kitten."

"Cat . . . there's nothing I can do. It's . . . it's too late."

"Is it?" My voice felt tight and funny. I let the clutch in and pulled away.

We took the area a block at a time and rang doorbells, going back to the empty places until we caught someone home. We didn't have a bit of luck tracing the car until six thirty when I had about four houses to go. A woman came by with an arm load of groceries, saw me getting into the car and stopped me. I had used a fake name all along and almost didn't hear her when she said, "Oh ... Mr. Wells . . ."

Anita pointed past me. "She's calling you, Cat."

"Yes?" I remembered her from one of the first calls.

"I was mentioning your visit to my husband when he came home. Well, it wasn't our car, but a friend of his who was staying overnight. He found his car damaged in the morning with the man's license number on his windshield."

"That's just fine, ma'm. We'd like to settle the matter as soon as possible, so if you can give me his name I'll get right to him."

"Certainly." She shifted her packages. "Jack Jenner . . . and he lives on Third Avenue North. He's in the book."

"Thank you. This has been a great help."

At the first pay station I stopped, looked up Jenner in the phone book and dialed his number. He seemed surprised to hear from me because so far he hadn't done anything about the incident. He read the license number out to me, I told him to process it as quickly as he could, thanked him and hung up.

One crack in the wall. That's all you need. There's always a chink somewhere that is the weakest point and can bring the whole structure down in ruins.

Anita said, "Have you found it?"

"Almost. There's a shadow figure in the picture and when the light hits we'll know for sure. Let's go back to my motel. I want to clean up and we can eat."

"I was supposed to see Vance. He'll . . ."

"He can wait. A kissin' cousin has some rights, hasn't he?"

"Uh-huh," she laughed, "but he'll be mad."

"What he needs is another poke in the mouth."

"He'll never forgive you for what you did to him."

"Tough. He was asking for it."

She nodded, not looking at me. "He's . . . always been like that. He had to fight his way up, you know . . . supported himself at school, started small in business and made everything the difficult way."

"What's new about that, kid? Someday I'll tell you my story."

I swung in at the motel and killed the engine. I opened the door, got one foot out when I saw the other car that was already nosed out start to move. The lights were off and if the top hadn't crossed the lights of the office I would have missed it. I yelled, "Down!" and gave Anita a shove that sent her on her back on the ground through the door on her side.

The blast of the gun came on top of the winking yellow light from the muzzle and a bullet smashed into the dashboard over my head sending glass fragments all over the place. I pulled the .45, thumbed the hammer back and let two go toward the car that was swerving in the gravel and heading back to town. From the angle I had to shoot I knew damn well that I had missed him, but they weren't sticking around for a shoot out. There could always be a second time.

I got Anita to her feet and inside as people came pouring out of their rooms. The clerk was shaking like a leaf, knocking on my door trying to find out what happened. I told everything was all right . . . it was an attempted stickup that didn't come off and nobody got hurt.

But I was wrong. He had called the police the minute he heard the shots and Lieutenant Travers himself answered the call. He came in with a uniformed sergeant, closed the door and stood there with his hands behind his back. "Mr. Bannerman . . . I assume you have a reasonable explanation for the shooting."

I told him the stickup story and he didn't go for it.

His smile was pretty grim. "You know," he said,

"I've had about enough of the Bannerman crap. They think they can get away with anything in this town and most of the times they can. I've been read off too often by my superiors who were under pressure and took too much lip from cheap politicians too many times. I think this time I'll nail me a Bannerman." His smile got colder with each word. "We had a complaint that you carry a gun. This so?"

There was no sense denying it. I nodded toward the chair where it lay under my coat.

Travers said, "Get it, Fred."

I knew what was coming next and started to get dressed. When I finished he said, "Let's go. All the talking you can do at headquarters with witnesses and someone to take your statement." He looked at Anita. "You too, miss."

Chapter 8

They sat us down around a table, my gun laying there in the middle and Travers looking pleased with himself. He had given Anita the opportunity to make a phone call and she got Vance Colby. He was on the way over.

In the meantime I made small talk, got the point across that I'd like some representation myself and after Travers thought it over he told the sergeant to plug in the phone. I got Wilkenson's name out of the book, told him who I was and where I was and asked him to get over fast. He was too excited to talk, but said he'd be there as quickly as possible.

For a ninety-three year old man he did a good job. He made it in five minutes. I hadn't seen him in twenty-five years and it looked as if he hadn't aged a bit. He was tall, topped with a bushy white head of hair, a manner that was positive and honest and it was easy to see why George P. Wilkenson was the most respected counsellor in the state.

We shook hands and his grip was firm. I was ready for a lot of gab, then got fooled there too. He asked Travers if he could speak to me alone for a few minutes and Travers was glad to grant him the courtesy. From his expression I knew what he was thinking . . . it would take a lot of talking to get me off the hook and it wasn't about to happen.

The tiny room we sat in stunk of stale sweat and cigar smoke and the edge of the table was notched with cigarette burns. I had seen too many of these rooms to enjoy being in one again. Wilkenson threw his briefcase on the table, pulled out a sheaf of papers and thrust them toward me, fanning them out so I could see the signature lines he had marked off.

"Cat," he said, "your father trusted me, so did your grandfather. Do you?"

"Why not?"

"Very well then." He held out a pen. "Sign where indicated."

I wrote my name in about twenty places, handed the pen back and stacked the papers together. "What was that all about?"

"Did you ever know the details of your grandfather's will?"

I made a noncommital gesture with my hands. "He split it with my old man and Miles, didn't he?"

"Up to a point, yes. There were certain other provisions. After their death the unspent capital would go to their children. If the children die, the remainder would go to the other brother or his children."

"So?"

"The final provision was this. Your grandfather knew your father's habits. It was his idea that his children might inherit his casual attitude of neglect and fail to claim the money. In that event, if the capital belonging to the deceased brother was not claimed by his children within thirty years, the others took possession. That time period is up . . . this Saturday. Tomorrow."

I still didn't get it. "Okay, so I inherit a hundred percent of nothing. Why all the business. The old man blew his load in a hurry. I hope he had fun."

"Ah, that's the point, son. He didn't. He was footloose enough, but his material possessions were very few. The fun he had didn't cost much at all. When he died he left quite a few million dollars intact. After taxes you stand to inherit at least two of them."

I felt my fingers bite the edge of the table and without realizing it I was on my feet. "*What?*"

166

Wilkenson nodded slowly. "That's why the urgency of having you sign the claim."

Now the picture was laid out from all angles. I asked the next question. "Where do Miles and his kids come in."

"Nowhere, I'm afraid. They have gone through every cent they ever had. You are the only wealthy Bannerman left."

"Damn!"

"But there's one clause that may disrupt everything, son. It has me worried. You stand to face a very serious charge."

"What about it?"

"Your grandfather was a peculiarly virtuous old man. He was honest and law abiding to the extreme. He specified in the will that if any of the inheritors should ever he held and booked by the police on a criminal charge, and found guilty, they were to be cut off immediately and the money transferred to the others."

No wonder the Bannermans were so fussy about keeping out of trouble. Buy anything or anybody, as long as the cost was less than the eventual one.

"Lieutenant Travers intends to book you. Carrying concealed weapons is a criminal charge."

"You let me take care of that," I said.

He shook his massive head. "I'm afraid he can't be bought."

"You let me take care of that," I repeated.

Wilkenson studied me a moment regretfully. He had done his duty, fulfilled his commitment, and now there was nothing more to do except make out more papers. I grinned at him, tight and nasty. "Don't count me out. Not yet. First do me a favor."

"If I can."

"Get hold of Petey Salvo." I gave him a list of places where he could be located. "Tell him to get Carl

Matteau and keep him with Gage until . . ." I looked at my watch, ". . . eleven o'clock tonight, then bring them to the Bannerman place. We'll be waiting."

He frowned at me. "But . . ."

"Just do it, okay?"

"Very well."

"Good. Now beat it. Don't let any of the others see you."

The sergeant took me back to the other room and there the clan was gathered; Miles, Rudy, Teddy and Vance. Anita had pulled away from him and looked at me anxiously when I came in and I didn't let my expression change at all. Except for Anita, they didn't seem a bit unhappy at all.

Vance said to Travers, "Now, sir, if it's all right with you, I would like to take Miss Bannerman home. It's been very trying for her."

The cop nodded agreement. "I know where to find her."

"Will there be any charges?"

"Oh, I don't think so," he said pleasantly. "She'll be a witness, naturally but as an innocent bystander. The one I want is right here." He pointed a long finger at me. I sat down and didn't look at them, but I managed a wink of confidence at Anita. She forced a smile, but her eyes were wet.

"Go on home, honey," I said. "It's not all that bad."

When they had gone Travers sat back, satisfied with himself, and said, "Now let's get to your statement."

I reached in my pocket and pulled out the license number I had gotten from the Jenner guy. "In the interests of harmonious relationships . . . and justice, how about finding out who owns the car that goes with this plate number."

He picked the slip from my fingers. "What kind of a game is this."

"Do it, then I'll tell you. You might get a promotion out of it."

Travers was a guy who enjoyed games. Besides, he couldn't understand my attitude. It had something to do with the way he smiled at me the last time.

He called the sergeant in, told him to run it through, then sat there saying nothing, idly tapping a pencil on the desk. I played the game with him for fifteen minutes until the sergeant came back with a card, handed it to Travers who looked at it, not getting what it meant, then handed it to me.

I said, "Touché. You get your promotion."

Then we had a little talk.

When it was over I picked up my gun, put it on and told Travers to follow me back to the Bannerman place with his sergeant and went out to the Ford.

Ten forty-five. The lights were on downstairs in the library and when I went in I could hear their voices. No longer were they tense . . . there was an air of relief and jocularity there now. Only Anita didn't have a drink in her hand and Vance Colby was standing in front of the desk like the old master himself, overshadowing Miles who held down his usual position. Rudy and Teddy were toasting each other and both were half still already.

They sobered up pretty fast when I came in. Their faces got a flat, sour look and Miles suddenly looked pale. Only Vance regained his composure. "We hardly expected to see you here."

"I guess you didn't." I walked over to Anita and sat on the arm of her chair. Her hand reached for mine, squeezed it and she bit her lip to keep from crying.

Then I played the time game on them, just sitting there silently. At eleven on the dot Petey Salvo came through the door holding Gage and Matteau by their necks. Matteau had taken a beating somewhere along the line and Popeye Gage was in the first stages of narcotics withdrawal. All he wanted was a fix and would do anything to get it while he had the chance. Later, when the cramps hit him, he wouldn't be able to.

"Pretty," I said. "Nice company the Bannermans keep."

Rudy had to sit down. I wouldn't let him. "On your feet, slob," I told him. "I want you to hear this standing up. I'm going to make you happy and sad all at once and I want to see what happens when I do."

"See here . . ." Vance started to say.

I waved a finger at him. "Not you, boy. You stay very, very quiet while I tell a story."

I said, "It started because this was a wide open state with legalized gambling and plenty of money to be made without too much work if the right deal could be swung. One man saw how he could do it. Cousin Rudy here made a sucker play for a ripe nympho named Irish Maloney and even if he didn't make out he established a motive for what was to come. The guy who spotted the move came into the family through a back door, knew what he was going to set up and made a contact with the Chicago Syndicate to borrow enough money to get his project rolling.

"The next step was easy. At the right time, when Rudy was drunk and sick, he got him to a toilet where he passed out, went outside and killed Chuck Maloney with a steak knife from the club, put the knife back, then had the Syndicate men put the word through that they had seen Rudy make the hit and that they had the evidence. *But all this while there was no evidence.*

"Then came the hitch . . . the money demand was going to fall through and how that must have shook up our killer. The Bannermans didn't have any loot left! Ah . . . but in a way, there was. Very shortly they were going to inherit my share of the wealth if I didn't claim it and there was little chance I would, so the killer was safe. A few more days and he'd have it made.

"Imagine how he felt when I showed up? Brother, he liked to 've browned out. The point was ... he had spent the Syndicate money on initial expenses and unless he got his hands on the Bannerman money he couldn't carry it through and he knew damn well the Syndicate wouldn't stand for the loss without getting something in return. Like his life.

"So our boy tried to have me roughed up and scared out by Gage and Matteau. They didn't want me dead ... just out of town long enough for the thirty year time period to expire. It didn't work. Now he got panicky. He even went as far as taking a shot at me himself. When that didn't work there was one other gimmick he had ready. He knew the details of the will and sent in a complaint that I carried a gun, a formidable charge if he could make it stick and one that would put my dough back in the hands of the other Bannermans. And three of them went for it. You know, I'm beginning to wonder just who the real bastard Bannermans are around here.

"Now our killer is really in a sweat because he doesn't know where I stand or what the next play is. He knows I have it locked but doesn't know how and has to hear me out to figure his next move.

"Funny how I found out about it. Real careless of him. He got the original idea because he liked the same dame Rudy liked and when he saw her under the phoney name of Arthur Sears she bragged about her men and up came the name of Rudy Bannerman ... and an ex con called Sanders. When they interrogate Sanders he'll tell them an anonymous call told him about Chuck's murder and that he's to be the first grabbed and the guy panicked. I bet that night he had even gotten drunk with some unknown guy and was carried home where he couldn't prove an alibi. But . . . that will come out later.

"Anyway, our Arthur Sears made a bad move. He backed into a car and drove off. An indignant dame saw it and grabbed his number. Only the number didn't belong to any Arthur Sears. The name that went with it was Vance Colby."

The glass dropped from his hands and he took an uncertain step back against the desk and stood there clutching it. Anita had me so tightly I couldn't move my arm, but it was my left one and didn't matter I could still draw and fire with my right.

"The dirty part was that you didn't give a damn about Anita, Vance. She wasn't your type. When your history gets checked out we'll find that out. All you wanted was the Bannerman money and when you had it you would have dumped her fast. Nice, dirty thinking."

From the doorway Carl Matteau was watching Colby with a face that was a hard mask. I said, "You have several choices, Carl. You probably have that gun on you that you shot at me with today. Move toward it and I'll kill you right where you stand. I'll put a .45 between your horns that will rip off the back of your head and spatter the old man there with more brains and blood than he already has.

"The second choice, Colby. You go out the back way and run for it. You'll have the cops on your back all the way, but it won't be them you'll be worrying about. It'll be the Syndicate boys because when Matteau here passes the word along a contract goes out on you and it will be worse than anything the cops can do to you.

"Third choice, killer. Outside the front door is a police car. You can get in, go downtown with Lieutenant Travers and hope the courts will give you life rather than the chair.

"Fourth choice is to brazen it out and if you look at Petey Salvo's face you'll see what can happen. Chuck

Maloney was his friend and Petey will go all the way for his buddies, dead or alive."

Vance Colby was dead white. There was no arrogance left in him now at all. He was a terrified animal with death facing him on all sides and all he could do was take the least of the evils. Very slowly he turned, looked at the open doors of the library to the hall beyond and started walking. He had company. Travers was back there and had heard it all. They went outside together and I heard the car start up and saw the red light on the top start to wink before they cleared the driveway.

I stood up and took Anita's hand. At the moment it was past her ability to comprehend, but soon she would see it. All she knew that somehow she suddenly belonged to me and me to her and the world was ours at last. The two little Bannermans who never meant anything because the others loomed too large and too powerful.

They weren't that way now. I said, "You're broke, cousins. You'll have to sweat for it now. You can have the house and the property but it'll make you even broker so you'll have to think fast. Personally, I don't think you'll survive long and you can blame it on yourselves. I want nothing you ever had and I'm taking what was mine and you tried to steal. You have to live with yourselves and it won't be easy, and while you do you can be thinking that the Bastard Bannerman wasn't the real bastard . . . it was you, the others. You're all bastards. I'm taking Anita out of here and I'll provide for Annie. I don't think she wants any part of you any more."

I pulled Anita toward the door and turned around. Rudy and Teddy had to sit down. It was too much for them. "Adios, Cousins and Uncle," I said. "Work hard and earn lots of money."

The night was clean, the sky peppered with stars and the road a moonlit ribbon heading east. She sat next to me as close as she could get and the radio played softly while I tooled along at an even sixty. Since we got married back there she had hardly spoken and I kept waiting for her to ask me.

She finally did. Curiosity, a trait of the Bannermans who bore the Cat label.

"That Lieutenant Travers . . . he let you go. What happened?"

"Nothing. I just told him who I was and where I was going. He checked on it."

"Are we going there now?"

"Uh-huh."

"Can you tell me?"

I looked at her and laughed. "It may interfere with our honeymoon, but it might be exciting at that. I'm picking up an escaped prisoner in New York and driving him back to the coast."

Amazement was written all over her. "But I thought you . . . you . . ."

"Police, doll. I was going east on a vacation and they let me have the assignment to save expenses."

"Oh, Cat . . ."

"Now I'll be like that millionaire cop on the TV show. Should be fun." I patted her leg and she snuggled up against me, warm and soft. "We'll have the honeymoon when we get back," I said.

THE END

A SELECTION OF FINE READING
AVAILABLE IN CORGI BOOKS

Novels

☐ FN	1467	A WALK ON THE WILD SIDE	Nelson Algren 5/–
☐ GN	7069	GIOVANNI'S ROOM	James Baldwin 3/6
☐ GN	7070	GO TELL IT ON THE MOUNTAIN	James Baldwin 3/6
☐ GN	7018	CATHERINE FOSTER	H. E. Bates 3/6
☐ GN	7003	LOVE HAS SEVEN FACES	Graeme Brewster 3/6
☐ FN	1278	THE GINGER MAN	J. P. Donleavy 5/–
☐ GN	7072	DUST IN MY THROAT	John Farrimond 3/6
☐ FN	1256	THE SONS AND THE DAUGHTERS	Patricia Gallagher 5/–
☐ FN	1502	THE COBWEB	William Gibson 5/–
☐ FN	7015	THE SURGEON	W. C. Heinz 5/–
☐ FN	1500	CATCH-22	Joseph Heller 5/–
☐ SN	7044	GUNS AT BATASI	Robert Holles 2/6
☐ FN	1489	STRANGERS WHEN WE MEET	Evan Hunter 5/–
☐ FN	7016	THE NEW INTERNS	William Johnston 5/–
☐ GN	1410	THE PHILANDERER	Stanley Kauffman 3/6
☐ FN	1455	SEVEN DAYS IN MAY	Knebel and Bailey 5/–
☐ FN	1394	THIS IS MY STREET	Nan Maynard 5/–
☐ GN	1505	NO MEAN CITY	McArthur and Long 3/6
☐ FN	1323	TALES OF THE SOUTH PACIFIC	James A. Michener 5/–
☐ EN	7045	HAWAII	James A. Michener 7/6
☐ FN	1066	LOLITA	Vladimir Nabokov 5/–
☐ EN	7054	PALE FIRE	Vladimir Nabokov 7/6
☐ FN	7030	THE BIG LAUGH	John O'Hara 5/–
☐ FN	1393	SERMONS AND SODA-WATER	John O'Hara 5/–
☐ FN	1484	ASSEMBLY	John O'Hara 5/–
☐ FN	1162	A STONE FOR DANNY FISHER	Harold Robbins 5/–
☐ FN	1187	79 PARK AVENUE	Harold Robbins 5/–
☐ FN	1202	NEVER LOVE A STRANGER	Harold Robbins 5/–
☐ SN	1204	NEVER LEAVE ME	Harold Robbins 2/6
☐ GN	1530	GOODBYE, COLUMBUS	Philip Roth 3/6
☐ EN	1529	LETTING GO	Philip Roth 7/6
☐ EN	1440	UHURU	Robert Ruark 7/6
☐ XN	1517	THE LIFE OF AN AMOROUS WOMAN	Ihara Saikaku 6/–
☐ FN	1487	THE DOCTORS	André Soubiran 5/–
☐ FN	7055	THE HEALING OATH	André Soubiran 5/–
☐ FN	1133	THE CARETAKERS	Dariel Telfer 5/–
☐ FN	1355	MILA 18	Leon Uris 5/–
☐ FN	7032	PLOUGH THE SEA	Robert Wilder 5/–
☐ FN	7068	WRITTEN ON THE WIND	Robert Wilder 5/–

War

☐ FB	7006	SEASON OF ESCAPE	James Allan Ford 5/–
☐ FB	7036	THE WILLING FLESH	Willi Heinrich 5/–
☐ FB	1490	THE CRUMBLING FORTRESS	Willi Heinrich 5/–
☐ GB	1461	THREE CAME HOME	Agnes Keith 3/6
☐ SB	1506	THE MAN WHO NEVER WAS	Ewen Montagu 2/6
☐ GB	1472	THE SCOURGE OF THE SWASTIKA	Lord Russell of Liverpool 3/6
☐ GB	1473	THE KNIGHTS OF BUSHIDO	Lord Russell of Liverpool 3/6
☐ GB	1538	633 SQUADRON	Frederick E. Smith 3/6
☐ FB	7071	THE MAN WHO PLAYED GOD	Robert St. John 5/–
☐ GB	7076	THE ANGRY HILLS	Leon Uris 3/6
☐ FB	1499	FACTORY OF DEATH	Vrba and Bestic 5/–

Romance

☐ GR	7065	THE YOUNG DOCTORS DOWNSTAIRS	Lucilla Andrews 3/6
☐ SR	7042	THE GREEN GRASS	Margaret Maddocks 2/6
☐ SR	7082	NURSE OFF CAMERA	Hilary Neal 2/6

Horror

- SN 7050 NO SUCH THING AS A VAMPIRE Ed. by Frederick Pickersgill 2/6
- SN 7048 FRANKENSTEIN Mary Shelley 2/6
- SN 7049 DR. JEKYLL & MR. HYDE and other macabre stories 2/6

Science Fiction

- GS 7082 NEW WRITINGS IN S.F.—I Ed. by John Carnell 3/6
- GS 7043 THE LAST LEAP Daniel F. Galouye 3/6
- GS 7066 THE SLEEP EATERS John Lymington 3/6
- FS 7028 A DECADE OF FANTASY AND SCIENCE FICTION Ed. by Robert P. Mills 5/–

General

- GG 1214 THE BRIDAL BED Joseph Braddock 3/6
- FG 1482 SEXUAL BEHAVIOUR Dr. Eustace Chesser 5/–
- FG 1498 LADY BEHAVE Edwards and Beyfus 5/–
- FG 7059 THE FINEST HOURS Jack le Vien and Peter Lewis 5/–
- FG 1513 MONEY ON YOUR MIND Richard Kellett 5/–
- FG 1542 THE CORGI BOOK OF GILBERT & SULLIVAN Ed. by Ross Lewis 5/–
- FG 7029 STATE OF EMERGENCY Fred Majdalany 5/–
- GG 7067 LIVING WITH THE LAMA T. Lobsang Rampa 3/6

Westerns

- F 683 BLOOD BROTHER Elliott Arnold 5/–
- SW 7040 HORSE HEAVEN HILL Zane Grey 2/6
- GW 7025 WANDERER OF THE WASTELAND Zane Grey 3/6
- GW 7064 NEVADA Zane Grey 3/6
- SW 1524 THE TRAIL DRIVER Zane Grey 2/6
- SW 7063 JOURNEY TO SHILOH Will Henry 2/6
- SW 7081 KIOWA TRAIL Louis L'Amour 2/6
- SW 7010 HANGING WOMAN CREEK Louis L'Amour 2/6
- GW 1436 THE SEARCHERS Alan Le May 3/6
- FW 1494 ORDEAL BY HUNGER George R. Stewart 5/–
- GW 1141 THE RANGE ROBBERS Oliver Strange 3/6

Crime

- SC 7021 BLOOD RUNS COLD Robert Bloch 2/6
- SC 7060 TERROR Robert Bloch 2/6
- GC 7037 DEEP FREEZE Jean Bruce 3/6
- SC 7061 MURDER IS FOR KEEPS Peter Chambers 2/6
- SC 7078 DEATH FROM BELOW John Creasey 2/6
- SC 7039 ROGUES' RANSOM John Creasey 2/6
- SC 7079 BEWARE THE CURVES A. A. Fair (Erle Stanley Gardner) 2/6
- GC 7038 TRY ANYTHING ONCE A. A. Fair (Erle Stanley Gardner) 3/6
- GC 7101 RETURN OF THE HOOD Mickey Spillane 3/6
- SC 1454 THE GIRL HUNTERS Mickey Spillane 2/6
- GC 1536 THE FLIER Mickey Spillane 3/6
- GC 7022 DEATH OF A TOM Douglas Warner 3/6
- SC 7023 DEATH OF A SNOUT Douglas Warner 2/6

All these great books are available at your local bookshop or newsagent; or can be ordered direct from the publisher. Just tick the titles you want and fill in the form below.

CORGI BOOKS, Cash Sales Department, Bashley Road, London, N.W.10.

Please send cheque or postal order. No currency, PLEASE. Allow 6d. per book to cover the cost of postage on orders of less than 6 books.

NAME ....

ADDRESS ....

(DE 64) ....